MW00974098

The time before the start of the invasion dwindled, as did the fear of my own death. I felt for Ouriel's knife strapped at my back, and the weight of it steadied me...

I didn't notice the demons until one had his arm clamped around my throat. Choking, I looked around and saw we were surrounded.

I didn't have to think before I reached for the knife at my back. Instinct and training took over, and I slammed my gift from Ouriel into the abdomen of the demon holding me. He dropped to the ground. I turned to stab him a few more times, to keep him out of the fight a bit longer, and then ran for Miriam and Ouriel. My sister was rapidly firing off arrow after arrow, sinking as many as left her quiver into demon flesh. But more kept popping in all around us.

I can't say how many demons I cut and sliced with my knife and nails to get to my sister and my Warrior, but I got through enough to guard their backs. Finally, the three of us stood back to back, facing down the enemy. Ouriel slipped me his knife, and both of my hands became deadly. Behind me and out of breath, he shouted, "Miriam, get Rose out of here! Run for Ishmael's house. I will cover you!"

"No way!" I yelled back. "I'm *not* leaving you!"

Ouriel decapitated two more of the demons rushing him. "You have to!"

"*No!*" I screamed and took down one of my own, kicking and jabbing her into a bloody pulp.

"We can't hold them all off," Miriam panted. "And I must save you at all costs."

Ouriel spun and, in one fluid move, gored a demon and pushed me through the opening toward Ishmael's house.

Born into a family of Guardians—extraordinarily gifted humans who protect mortal souls—seventeen-year-old Rose Kazin shows no signs of being blessed with the supernatural talents her family has used for generations to fight demons. When she and her father figure, an age old celestial Warrior, are horribly wounded in a demonic ambush, Rose awakens to find a younger Warrior, Ouriel, has volunteered to stand in as her protector. She rails against his presence—and her own heart—but Ouriel seems interested in only one thing: teaching Rose how to protect herself from the demons she was never supposed to fight.

KUDOS for *The Broken*

In The Broken by Julia Joseph, Rosa Kazin is like the ugly duckling. In a family of fierce Guardians, fighting for good against evil demons, Rosa is the no-talent, strictly human little sister. When her protector, the ancient Warrior Ishmael, is badly injured, trying to protector from demons, Rosa is assigned a new protector, Ouriel, a much younger, more dashing Warrior. Whereas Ishmael was like a father to Rosa, Ouriel is something of a hunk and Rosa is smitten. But Ouriel is only interested in training Rosa to protect herself. Or is he? I must say that for a debut novel, The Broken is an excellent effort. The book is very well written, the characters well-developed and charming, and the plot is strong. The Broken is one you will want to keep on your shelf to read over and over again. – *Taylor Jones, Reviewer*

The Broken by Julia Joseph is a rather-sophisticated YA novel about angels and demons and the war between good and evil. That seems to be a fairly common theme for YA authors these days. Joseph's characters are three-dimensional and well-developed. I liked the fact that Rosa seemed to be the one flawed member of an otherwise awesome Guardian family. But unlike most of us, who would be complaining that we didn't get the same Gifts as the rest of the family, Rosa is okay with this. She doesn't really want to fight world-changing battles with dark forces. She just wants to live in peace. Unfortunately, Rosa's hopes are shattered when it turns out that she isn't quite the no-talent wimp she thought she was. For a first-time author, I think Joseph has a real winner here. I, for one, am hungrily looking forward to the next one in the series. – *Regan Murphy, Reviewer*

ACKNOWLEDGEMENTS

First, I want to thank my husband, my children, and my entire family—without all of your support, I could never have accomplished any of this.

I'd also like to thank the many friends and battle buddies who have kept me sane through the last eleven years of being an Army wife.

Last, but definitely not least, I must thank the Red Pen Warriors—you all rock!

THE
BROKEN

BY

JULIA JOSEPH

A Black Opal Books Publication

GENRE: YA/PARANORMAL THRILLER/PARANORMAL ROMANCE

THE BROKEN
Copyright © 2014 by Julia Joseph
Cover Design by Joseph Brooks
All cover art copyright © 2014
All Rights Reserved
Print ISBN: 978-1-626941-04-5

First Publication: JANUARY 2014

Published by Black Opal Books **http://www.blackopalbooks.com**

DEDICATION

*For my mother and grandmother,
the two greatest women I will ever know—*

*Without you, I would not be the woman I am today.
Thank you. I love you. I will miss you both
every day for the rest of my life.*

PROLOGUE

Demons were all around us. Most people just didn't know because they disguised themselves well.

I was born into a family of Guardians—humans gifted with extraordinary powers by the Creator Himself—so I had always known that ours was a world at war. Not the "wars" you'd see on the news or in papers, but a never-ending, vicious struggle between the few who could See and the demons who would devour us all…

❦❦❦

As it had for the last thirteen years of my life, the nightmare plagued me yet again, and I couldn't hide from the ugly scene that played out in my mind. Heavily outnumbered, my parents fought a bloody and ferocious battle for their souls.

No one heard my scream as I watched my mother and father fall into the bloody pool from which they could never return.

CHAPTER 1

I woke up Friday morning, sweating and panicked after a night spent reliving my parents' deaths. It had been years since I'd last had to suffer the torment of that particular nightmare and, of course, the sheer exhaustion of the ordeal caused me to oversleep. I fought the overwhelming urge to roll over, bury myself under the covers, and ignore the demands of my life. I could hear from their movements that my sisters were already up and about, so I knew I had to move too, whether I felt like it or not. I really hated getting up on mornings like these. I was just so tired. Tired of trying, every day, to be someone I wasn't and do what was expected of me— living in one world but belonging to another.

"Hurry up, Rose! You're going to be late. *Again*. Ishmael will be here any minute," Miriam, my oldest sister, called from the kitchen.

I fought the urge to stay in bed just to spite her. She'd always been so "with it," so organized. It was really disgusting. I stifled a snort, thinking about how she'd smack me for that insult if I'd said it where she could hear me. Groaning, I decided to get up. If I didn't, Ishmael would be disappointed in me, and I *really* hated that.

I dragged myself into the bathroom and shoved my exhausted body into the shower. I tried not to sink back into a stupor, but the warm water nearly lulled me into a coma.

"Ishmael's here!" Genevieve, my other sister, chimed as she cracked the bathroom door open. Her voice was like cold water, splashing me back into the present with a jolt. "And he doesn't look very happy."

"Get out!" I hissed back and rifled a bar of soap at her. She ducked neatly and closed the door as the soap slammed against the doorjamb just beyond where her face had been. *I may be Sightless, but I've got great aim*! I thought to myself. Unfortunately, that didn't sound so impressive if you happened to know that, in my world, being Sightless had nothing whatsoever to do with how well your eyes worked.

Still, I was pleased with my small demonstration of skill and sailed through the rest of my routine. I slapped my soaking-wet, blonde hair up into a ponytail and didn't stop to camouflage my unabashedly Middle Eastern features with makeup. Why draw attention to eyes that were the weirdest shade of blue ever to exist in the natural world, anyway? I had no one to impress.

Rather than spare my reflection a second glance, I dashed out of the bathroom, grabbed my backpack from the kitchen table at full speed—and ran smack into Ishmael. He didn't budge, but I fell flat on my back. I found myself suddenly eyeing a work boot and the pant leg of a custodian's set of overalls.

"You really are something, my darling *Rousa*," Ishmael chuckled as he picked me up with one hand and set me on my feet. His piercing green eyes scanned me for injuries, and his already wrinkled face cracked into a huge grin when he was satisfied that I remained unharmed. "My dear, I simply cannot keep creating excuses for why we are so often late. This is the second time this week, and school has only recently resumed."

"I'm sorry, Ishmael. I was up late last night studying," I fibbed easily.

"*Rousa!*" Ishmael chastised, using, as he always did, the original Arabic form of my name. "You know very well that some Warriors can sense lies. You also know that I am one of them. However, I do not need that ability now to know that you are not telling the truth. You never study." He chuckled again.

"I had to try, didn't I?" I attempted to look guilty. I knew that I couldn't get a fib past Ishmael, but I had a good reason to try. I needed to keep up a lighthearted appearance because I didn't want him to find out what I'd really been doing. He didn't need to know the nightmare had returned after all this time. He'd only worry about me more.

Sometimes, I truly hated the super sensory skills of Warriors.

One of my few natural talents was lying, but it never served me well with Ishmael. "You know, Ish, the way you talk, a person would think you're my father, not my protector," I grumbled.

Ishmael ignored my attempt to goad him into a mood as surly as mine. "I swore an oath the day your parents died that I would protect you for the rest of your earthly life. Coming to feel as though I am your father has been a surprisingly sweet benefit. Come now, into my arms, and I will Jump us to school, seeing as we will not arrive in time by human means."

I didn't bother to hide my sudden excitement. I loved being Jumped from one place to another by Ishmael. He rarely did it, for fear of being caught by the Sightless, and I often tarried in the mornings to make it necessary. It had become our routine during the first three years I had been forced to attend a Sightless school. In fact, the only thing I cherished about my trips to and from school was the opportunity to be with Ishmael.

And, despite my silly complaints, I was very thankful that Ish had become a father figure to me in the years since my mother and father had been ripped so brutally from my sisters and me. A shiver slid through my body. Any fleeting thought of my parents caused me excruciating pain and, instinctively fleeing the agony, I ran into Ishmael's waiting arms. Denying the suffering which always seemed to be waiting, just a step behind to devour me, had become my default way of dealing with life. I pressed my face into the amber colored skin of Ish's neck, and his scent comforted me—just as I'd known it would.

I forced my thoughts back into the present and steeled myself for the coming Jump. No matter how often I traveled this way, I had never grown accustomed to it. I remembered to scream, "Bye Miri! Bye Gen! Love you!" just before I felt my body melt into nothingness. Before I could gasp for more air, Ish and I solidified again about two miles from my house behind a shed in someone's backyard.

He checked briefly to make sure we hadn't been seen, and I took a desperate breath. "Are you ready for the next one?" he asked.

I nodded and we dissolved again. This time, we re-formed in the janitor's closet at school—Ishmael's "office," as he liked to call it. He'd worked for the last three years as a custodian at my high school in order to be near me. The job provided him with a cover and me with a discounted tuition rate. Thankfully, only my senior year kept him from his real retirement, and it had already begun. I wasn't sure how he felt about it, but I was going to be glad to be done with the whole charade in a few months.

"I wish you weren't such a good Jumper," I puffed as we landed. "Shouldn't it take most Warriors at least four Jumps to make it this far?"

"Yes, my dear. Most of them. It is unfortunate that not everyone can be as efficient as I."

I giggled at his boast, kissed him on the cheek, and ruffled his shock of white hair before I straightened my blue-plaid, uniform skirt and white sailor top. Leaving Ishmael to prepare for his morning, I waltzed out of the room like I'd been in there doing last minute homework.

Kids were already filling the halls with early morning chatter, so I made for my locker. It didn't take long to get there, as it was a small co-ed Catholic high school of about 250 students. We had two floors with about six classrooms each and only one indoor stairwell. From the front office, we had a great view of the fence surrounding the El Paso Zoo. On windy days—which most were in this big dusty city—we had the added benefit of being directly downwind of the elephants' enclosure. The taste of dirt and elephant dung made a lovely contribution to much of my time at school.

If I had been of a Sightless family, Father Yermo would have been a good place to get an education. For me, however, the place felt like a jail. I wanted to scream myself free of such unnecessary Sightless customs. Unfortunately for me, I *was* Sightless, and I needed to come to terms with that little detail. I would never be a full Guardian like my sisters. Nothing would ever change the fact that I couldn't See. I would never have the kind of gifts my sisters and other Guardians used to battle evil. As Gen always said, it was better to make peace with what I was than to fight it.

Sighing, I opened my locker and got out the books I needed for class. I only carried my backpack for show when I went home. There was never anything of substance in it.

I made it to first period just in time and gritted my teeth through the tedious morning announcements. When those were finished, Mrs. Palmer immediately went to work enumerating the many faults of Andrew Jackson and his Indian Removal policy, and I felt my mind slide into semi-consciousness. It's not that she wasn't a great teacher. She was my favorite, but I'd pretty much achieved the Guardian equivalent of a high school diploma by the age of twelve. Most of my school days felt like a review of what I'd already learned years earlier.

It had been Miriam's idea that I join the Sightless world when my lack of the Gift became too evident to ignore. She said I needed "to adjust to a 'regular' life, and what better way to do that than attend high school?" I kicked and screamed for weeks in protest, but I'd never really had a choice. Doing what was expected of me, no matter the personal cost, ran in my Guardian blood, whether I could See or not. And so there I was, dutifully stuck in a place I really didn't want to be.

Lunchtime came quickly, and I kept to myself in the cafeteria—as always. I thought for a moment about sneaking off to eat with Ishmael, but I changed my mind. Everybody at Father Yermo High School believed he was my father, and teenage girls weren't supposed to like hanging out with their dads. I supposed they felt I should have been embarrassed to admit my father was the school custodian in the first place, much less that he was also my best friend. After the night I'd had, I wasn't in the mood to listen to any of their thinly veiled insults about my lack of interest in being social. As if I had a real choice in the matter, considering my unorthodox home life.

Instead of seeking refuge with Ishmael, I gulped down my lunch and ran off to the library to read for the last twenty minutes before afternoon classes. I rejoiced in the quiet solitude and hated to get up when the bell rang. Luckily for me though, the rest of the day passed in a blur, and I was heading back to Ishmael's "office" before I knew it.

After the final bell, I usually hung out for an hour or so while Ish puttered around pretending to be working hard at getting the school clean. It always amazed the faculty and staff that he finished his work so quickly and efficiently. He never missed a thing—his school was spotless. None of them ever guessed that there was some-thing supernatural about his amazing competence.

Ish winked at me as he went by, with jingling keys, for his last pass of the dust mop in the hallway. I smiled to myself and shook my head at the things the Warrior was willing to do to in the name of keeping me safe. Not that I would be, or had ever been, in any *actual* danger. But I'd never been taught to defend myself, so Ishmael insisted on always being around when I left the safety of my house. Why a being so powerful would consent to leading the life he did, just to be near me, I didn't really understand, but I *was* grateful, if only for his companion-ship. I led a very lonely life that included few people. Re-alizing that Ishmael was almost ready to leave, I forced myself to focus on what little homework I had left. I finished it quickly and stowed my things in my locker.

"I am now ready, *Rousa*." Ishmael walked up as I slammed the metal door shut. "We will return home in the truck. I retrieved it earlier today, so it is already in the lot."

I groaned. I hated that thing. The truck was a loud, rumbling, burnt orange 1972 GMC that had belonged to my grandfather. It was, in my mind, a serious embarrassment to any female forced to ride in it. I hid my grimace and headed for the door, waiting only for Ish to lock up behind us.

As we meandered across the parking lot, I noticed how out of place Ishmael looked, walking next to me. It seemed outrageous that most humans didn't recognize the preternatural beauty that shone from within him. How could anyone *not* know what he was? It also became clear to me what he must have sacrificed over the years in order to stand as my protector. The magnitude of the act nearly overwhelmed me.

Rather than embarrass Ishmael with a sappy comment of some sort, I opted for sarcasm. "You know, Ish, this really is a crappy way to spend your retirement—hanging out with humans and cleaning up after a bunch of thankless teenagers."

"It is not as bad as it may seem. Besides, Warrior retirement can last decades, sometimes centuries." He paused to smirk at me. "And although it pains me to admit it more than once daily, I must say that becoming a part of your life has made it *somewhat* worthwhile."

I picked up on my cue to begin a new round of our continual sarcastic banter with some sort of sassy retort, but a strange sensation burning its way down the back of my neck shocked me into silence. I tried to brush the feeling off with my hand, but it spread up my scalp and down my spine. Feeling slightly panicky, I turned to Ishmael for reassurance. Our eyes met. In his was a blazing green inferno.

I had only seen his eyes rage like that one time before.

The night my parents died.

Ishmael began to glow and, even the bright sunlight, I could see green flames licking their way along the skin of his arms and hands. I knew we were in extreme danger. Ishmael grabbed me from behind, attempting to Jump with me. Before he could, demons Jumped in all around us. He tried to shield me from them with his body, but I could still see their horrible faces, each twisted with its own brand of evil.

I hadn't seen many demons in my sheltered lifetime, but these looked especially vicious. Only one had wings, so I knew that she had to be the leader. The others still looked almost human, except for the sickly tinge of their skin and their sharp nails and teeth.

I felt like vomiting.

"What do you want, demoness?" Ishmael demanded, his furious power clearly evident in his voice.

"Don't worry, Warrior. It is not you we have come for. We want the human," the winged female replied, brushing matted, bloody hair back from her face.

"You will not have her. She is useless to you anyway. She is Sightless."

The demoness licked her lips with menace. "She is of Guardian blood. We must have her."

I tried not to allow my mind to melt into fear. When I looked directly at her, it seemed as if the demon's face shifted—like she took on some of my features. I closed my eyes in an attempt to banish the image before it burned itself into my brain.

When I opened them again, I saw Ishmael searching out and rejecting our alternate routes of escape. I couldn't see any way out. There were at least five demons, and without me to hinder him, Ishmael could have dealt with them easily. He couldn't leave me unguarded long enough to fight off all of them. My useless damsel-in-distress self was the mother of all distractions in a brawl.

The demons closed in on us, inhaling our scent. Their stench was vile—like rotting flesh. My body frozen, I fought to retain control of my mind. I wanted to scream out to Ishmael, "Just let them have me! Save yourself!" But I knew he would die rather than let them take me. And *that* thought finally spurred me into action.

I pretended to faint. I dropped like a rock, surprising Ishmael into loosening his grip on me. As soon as I felt him release me, I sprang away from my protector and threw myself at the female leader. I tackled her and, not knowing what else to do, tried to rip the hair off her head.

I heard the fight break out behind me as the other demons rushed at Ishmael. All I could think was, *I can't lose him too. I can't*...and I fought ever harder against my demon. I knew I couldn't win, but I continued kicking and scratching. I let out a scream as she landed a well-placed blow on my temple. It took all I had to remain conscious.

Dazed, I clawed at her eyes with my nails. I felt her putrid flesh tearing under my attack, but she clamped her arms in a vice around my chest, crushing the air out of my lungs. We both felt the fight leaving my body as she tried to take flight and Jump away with me. I knew I was lost, but I felt only relief. At least Ish would be safe.

Something seemed to go wrong with the demoness's attempt at flight. I must have injured her wings at some point because she couldn't seem to gain enough clearance for the Jump. Her arms loosened around me, allowing hot, dry desert air to burn its way down my throat and into my suffocating lungs. The return of oxygen to my body cleared my vision in time to witness Warriors and Guardians Jumping in everywhere before I blacked out.

കൃകൃ

"Ishmael!" was the first thought that came to my mind as I awoke. I didn't realize I had screamed his name aloud until I heard Miriam's reply.

"He's alive. He was hurt pretty badly trying to fight his way to you, but he'll be fine. Warriors heal quickly. Rest now."

I felt the darkness reclaim me, but my mind continued to yearn for Ishmael…

e⁄ɔe⁄ɔ

I was in a dark room. The only light came from a pool glowing blood red in the center of the floor. I tried hard not to look at it too closely. I had seen this room many times before in my nightmares, but this time it was different. I was actually in the room, not just observing from afar. It all felt much too realistic. Still, I knew the routine well. My parents were coming.

Wake up! *Wake up*! I thought frantically but I knew, once the nightmare had started, I would be forced to watch it all over again. In horrific detail. I knew the demon was lying in wait for my parents.

"Where is she?" It seemed my father appeared out of nowhere. He was carrying his sword, looking as young and handsome as the last time I had seen him. But I was confused. This wasn't how it usually happened in my dreams. Before, their voices had been muted, and I could only see the action and try to guess at their words.

This time, I heard a silky voice reply, "Who?"

"Where is our daughter, demon?" My mother's voice was not soft and sweet now, as it was when she sang me to sleep. It sounded flinty and commanding. "We know you have her, Ausen."

"You are mistaken. It seems you have made this trip in vain. As you can see, I do not have your daughter in my possession." Ausen stepped into the eerie red glow of the pool. I shivered, as I always did, when I saw him. He was humanoid in form but grotesquely misshapen. He had the characteristic demonic green tint to his skin. His teeth were viciously sharp and his gums black.

His bald head and greenish-gold eyes reminded me of a rattlesnake. Dim memories of my Guardian education told me that he was a somewhat high-ranking demon. He hadn't yet earned talons for his feet, but he did have bat-like wings.

My mother nocked an arrow in her bow.

"There is no need to be so aggressive, Najla, dear girl. Put down your weapon." Ausen's voice sounded more patronizing than conciliatory.

"I will ask one more time," my father cut in. "Where is our daughter, Ausen?"

"As I said before, I do not have her. However, I am willing to negotiate a price for her. Allow me to show you." With a nod of Ausen's head, more demons slithered out of the shadows around the room. They outnumbered my parents ten to one. "You see, the daughter you believed lost has just been located and is now in the custody of a single Warrior. If you agree to have her brought to me, I will allow you to live."

"You honestly believe we will give up without a fight?" my father boomed.

My mother threw back, "We would never trade her for our lives! Only a monster would consider that possible."

"Then you will die, and I will have her anyway." Ausen flew up into the air and his minions attacked. The last image in my mind, as I clawed my way into consciousness, was my parents falling—falling into the pool of blood.

ℰᔆℰᔆ

My mind returned to consciousness slowly, and I struggled to retain snatches of the whispered conversations taking place at my bedside. "She's been reliving that nightmare…" How did they know that? "…what to do for her…" Those few words urged me to struggle harder to keep my mind from floating back into the darkness. "…the same one from right after our parents died." Finally, I recognized Miriam's voice.

Unfortunately, the one voice I wanted to hear more than any other remained absent. My fear for Ishmael did what I alone couldn't. I quickly regained consciousness, only to have a bolt of guilt shoot through me for any damage he had suffered because of me. It must have been serious because nothing else would have kept him from my bedside.

"I don't think there's anyone who can help her, sweetheart," the voice of Miriam's husband, Shadrach, came in clearly now.

"But I've seen that nightmare of hers in my dreams. I don't know how she lives with it. If she—" Miriam broke off.

Another voice, unfamiliar but oddly comforting, cut in, "She is awake. It is best you stop."

All three beings in the room looked at me. Miriam, with her reddish brown curls, was perfection as always, but her sea blue eyes were clouded with worry. Shad's dark brow furrowed with frustration, and his brown eyes still shone fiercely from the earlier fight. The other man was beyond description. I guessed that he was a Warrior because his telltale amber skin glowed with a soft incandescence in my darkened bedroom.

I didn't know how old he was. He appeared very young, nineteen or twenty, but it was impossible to tell a

Warrior's true age. And, like other Warriors, he was marvelous in appearance, with long auburn hair that laid flat against his back. Two braids parted it from the center and were neatly tucked behind his ears.

The Warrior's eyes blazed a dark blue with a kind of fire simmering in them. *Oh goodness,* I thought, *he is just...beyond words.* I tried to smack myself out of my silent stare, but I couldn't seem to drag my eyes away from him.

My reaction to the Warrior unsettled me. I tried, and failed spectacularly, to cover my momentary loss for words. In an attempt to calm down, I told myself that the unknown Warrior's effect on me was a natural one, considering I'd seen very few of them, especially young ones, in my lifetime. Despite that, I still wasn't able to speak, and I decided that I lacked the social skills necessary to deal with a stranger in my current mental condition.

I hope that stupid demon didn't damage my brain permanently. Holy crap. I can't even gather my thoughts enough to ask his name.

Probably sensing my question, he stepped forward. "If I may," he murmured with a slight bow. "I am Ouriel. I have fought alongside your sisters and Shadrach since they were of age. I hope my presence here does not disturb you."

Of course his presence disturbed me! How could it not? Flushing, I forced out a few words. "N—No. It's, um, it's f—fine. Really. Do you happen know anything about Ishmael?"

"No, I am sorry." Ouriel's face tightened, and he swept from the room, leaving me gawking after him from my bed.

"Um—who exactly was that?" I asked Miriam when my tongue could move again.

"Shad, maybe you should let me explain. I want Rose to understand. Do you think…" Miriam let her question drift off midsentence and allowed Shad to fish it out of her mind. I really hated when they did that. It was annoying to listen to only half of a conversation.

"Believe me, I would rather not be in here for this," he replied, wincing. "Just remember what Ouriel said." Shad kissed Miriam and slipped out the door, closing it with a hushed click.

"What was all that about? What's going on? How is Ishmael? Why were those demons after us?" I couldn't seem to stem my flood of questions until Miriam finally answered.

"I don't know what I should tell you, exactly," she began, "but it does seem that you are going to need more protection after today. Our intelligence tells us there's been some kind of turbulence among the demon hierarchy. It doesn't bode well. And Ishmael is going to be out of commission for a while."

"*What*? Is he okay? How long will he be gone? And who's going to take his place? You or Genevieve?"

"Um—well…the healers say he will be okay but his recovery is going to be difficult and take some time. And Genevieve and I can't protect you as well as a Warrior." Miriam looked like she dreaded what she had to say next.

What didn't she want to tell me? "So—Ouriel has volunteered to stand in and stay as long as he's needed."

"Ouriel? That Warrior who was just in here?"

"Yes. He's going to enroll at school with you and pretend to be a new student there."

"Miriam, there's no way! People will figure it out. Seriously, have you looked at the guy? Does he know what he's going to be in for, hanging around all those Sightless teenage girls?" I couldn't believe it. I didn't want some strange Warrior protecting me. I was *not* good with new people. Besides, how would we explain away some gorgeous male specimen following me around school all the time?

"Ouriel is a top-ranking Warrior. You can't have better protection than that. And he knows what he's doing."

"Still! Do I really need him? Couldn't you or Shad just take me to school?" I tried to keep the petulance out of my voice, but I'd suddenly turned into a disgustingly sulky teenager. And my independent nature balked at the idea of Ouriel tailing me. I wanted Ishmael. "Miriam, I don't need a new protector! You guys are overreacting. We can make do until Ish is better. And I seriously think those demons must have confused me with someone else. There is no way it could have been me they were really interested in."

"For some reason we don't know, Rose, those demons *were* after you today. If I hadn't been so tired that I had to take a quick nap this afternoon, I don't know what would have happened…" Miriam's voice trailed off and a strange expression clouded her face. She looked a little guilty, and I thought I knew why.

"You dreamed it didn't you? I wondered how all those Guardians and Warriors showed up so fast."

She nodded. "I was so scared. I didn't know if I was Seeing what had already happened or if it was just then happening."

"Speaking of which, did any Sightless see what happened? Did you have to send in a clean-up crew?" I tried to contain a shiver. Most battles in the Endless War remained unseen, as both sides had a vested interest in remaining undetected. Sometimes, though, when an errant human wandered into something they shouldn't, clean up teams were called in. They consisted of people skilled in the art of manipulating people's memories—an art most Guardians found unnerving but necessary.

"Thankfully, no. You left so late, the parking lot and street were already deserted—" Miriam stopped short. "I thought I was going to lose you. When I got there and saw that demoness trying to take off with you—well—I went a little crazy. I can't believe you went after her like that! Why didn't you let Ishmael handle her?"

"I'm sorry, Miri. But I just couldn't let Ishmael die protecting me. I had to at least try—"

"No!" Miriam shouted. "It wouldn't have been your fault! We all go into battle willingly and would just as willingly die to keep each other safe. You cannot allow guilt to give a demon the advantage. Do you understand me?"

I had never seen her so angry. "I'm sorry, Miriam. Really. Don't be mad at me. Please." She didn't look satisfied with my apology, but, now that I knew that Ishmael was going to live, something else clamored for attention in my mind. "Listen, there's something else I want to talk to you about. I don't know what to think about it, but…" I didn't know how to explain the new developments in my nightmare.

"What is it?"

"Well, I know you have Seen my nightmare with Mom and Dad before in your dreams. And just now, while I was unconscious, I had the stupid thing again. Only, this time, it changed. It was different."

"It was different? How?"

"Well, instead of watching the scene from far away, I was actually there, but that's not all. Before, I could never hear what they were saying, but, tonight, I heard everything…" I trailed off when I saw that Miriam's face had become guarded.

She leaned toward me. "What did you hear?"

"Well, Mom and Dad kept asking this demon—this Ausen—for their daughter. For one of us, I guess. They never said which one. I just figure it was you because you were the only one of age at the time—" I stopped short, starting to feel stupid. Why would any of this matter? It wasn't like my dreams meant anything. I had never Seen anything and these nightmares, as Miriam had told me time and again, were just my mind trying to make sense of what had happened to my parents. I knew they had been killed in a battle with a powerful demon, but there was no way to know anything else. Their bodies had never been found, and it was rumored the demon had died along with them. "I'm sorry I brought it up, Miri. It's dumb."

"No, honey, it's not. That night haunts me, too. I *had* just come of age remember? I'd looked forward to fighting alongside them for so long—" Miriam's eyes glazed over. She shuddered and seemed to shake something off. "We still don't know much about that night. I'm sure that these new developments in your nightmare are just your way of dealing with what happened tonight. What we need to do is forget the past and try to figure out why someone would want to hurt you now."

I didn't want to tell her that I believed her worrying was useless. I was of next to no importance to anyone besides her, Genevieve, and Ish. The attempted kidnapping could never have been meant for me. Instead, I pretended to look exhausted. Thankfully, that wasn't very hard.

"Okay. But, before you go, Miriam, tell me more about Ishmael. Please. Is he really going to be okay?"

"As far as we know right now, Rose, he *is* going to live. I don't know how severe his injuries are just yet because I've been so worried about you, but I will try to find out for you."

"Thanks, Miri. I love you." I almost couldn't get the words out. My heart broke with anxiety for Ishmael, and silent tears snaked their way down my face and onto my pillowcase.

"Love you too, baby."

Miriam knelt at my bedside and hugged me fiercely, leaving me to return the embrace with more than a twinge of guilt because I yearned only for Ishmael's touch.

CHAPTER 2

I woke up after noon the next day—a Saturday—thankful that I didn't even need to think about school. Even though my head pounded as I shuffled to the bathroom, my reflection in the mirror still shocked me. I had taken quite a beating the night before. It amazed me that I'd even made it out of the fight alive.

A deep gash slanted from the hairline just above my right temple to below my cheekbone, and, from the stitches, I could tell a Guardian healer had come by sometime during the night while I lay unconscious. I also sported two attractive black eyes that were not really black at all, but ranged in a spectacular starburst of colors from yellow to green to purple, and two broken ribs—as Miriam had explained to me only minutes before when I'd tried to hobble past her in the hallway.

None of that really mattered at the moment, however, because I still couldn't seem to cope with Miriam's revelation that Ishmael was seriously injured. The miniscule amount of information she'd been able to procure detailed only that he was under the constant care of a specialized team of Guardian and Warrior healers who fully expected him to recover. It had taken all of my patience not to scream down the house when I realized she had nothing better in her update for me, and even more so when she told me no one was allowed to see him yet.

I finished washing up and heard the doorbell chime its shockingly loud notes throughout our silent house.

"Do you feel like getting that, Rose?" Genevieve called from her room down the hall. "Please? I know you're up. Miriam just left for her patrol, and I'm swamped right now!"

"Oh, sure. *I'll* get it. It's not like I almost died last night or anything," I grumbled as I limped painfully to the door. Gen was shut up in her room again, too busy talking to all the things she Saw to be bothered. Hers was a truly strange and rare Gift. I didn't really understand it, other than knowing that she constantly received visits from spirits or entities of some sort. Pushing aside my irritation, I grabbed the knob of the front door and yanked it open, only to be rewarded with a screaming protest from my ribs. When I saw who waited, not-so-patiently, on the front porch, I felt my grimace of pain melt into one of shock and embarrassment.

Ouriel seemed just as surprised to see me answering the door as I'd been to find him on the other side of it. With the sun burning red into his dark hair, the Warrior looked even younger than he had the night before.

Dressed in jeans, T-shirt, and a pair of tennis shoes, I thought for a moment that Ouriel might actually have a chance at passing for a Sightless teenaged human, at least until I noticed the enormous sword strapped to his back. I fought the urge to laugh at the sight he made, modern and archaic, all jumbled into a disgustingly attractive, seemingly natural whole.

"Should you be up, answering doors after last night?" he asked. "You look dreadful."

Ouch! That comment knocked the mirth right out of me. It struck me that Ouriel might be more socially backward than I was—if that was even possible. He obviously didn't mince words either.

"Thanks," I shot back. "Please come on in and feel free to insult me some more. I find it makes for the best kind of small talk. While you're at it, when Genevieve is finally finished talking to all her spirit buddies, she'd probably love to join you."

I knew my response sounded combative, but I couldn't control myself. I also wasn't above placing the blame for it on Ouriel. No one should ever tell a girl she looks "dreadful."

"I am certainly sorry to have offended you. I was merely shocked to see you up so soon after the trauma you endured last night." Ouriel's words dripped with sarcasm.

"That's not much of an apology." I needed to learn to control my attitude, but I just couldn't stop. "Have you ever heard the saying, 'Adding insult to injury'? Oh— who cares? I think I'll just go back to bed before you grind down my ego anymore." I stalked, as well as I could manage in my condition, back to my room, and slammed the door, all while grumbling, "You'd think, as old as he must be, he'd know…"

I had just snuggled under the covers of my bed when I heard a hesitant knock on my bedroom door. "Rose, I *am* sorry for offending you." Ouriel's deep voice reverberated through the thin wood. "May I please speak with you? I know you are not feeling well, but may I come in? I will try to be more polite and not—what was it you said?—add any more insults to your numerous injuries."

I groaned. Was I just destined to suffer this weekend? And did I hear a grin lurking behind his polite words? Surely not. He didn't seem capable of humor. "If I let you talk to me, will it make you go away any quicker?" My head pounded even louder.

"Pardon me?"

"Never mind," I said as politely as I could under the circumstances. "Just come in."

Ouriel opened the door, and it did look as if a smile ghosted about his face. When he reached my bedside, however, he wore the same remote expression I remembered groggily from the night before.

"I am sorry to disturb you." He shifted from foot to foot at the end of my bed. "I actually came here to speak with Miriam. However, I believe it is fortuitous that you answered the door and she is away. I feel it may serve my purpose better to speak to you directly. There are matters we need to settle before you return to school Monday."

"Before you start with all that, do you have any news on Ishmael? Is he any better?"

Ouriel shook his head somberly. "I am sorry to report that his condition is still critical. The Healers seem certain he will survive, but his body has suffered damage so severe that they are having great difficulty in alleviating his pain. I wish I could give you a more detailed update, but they were quite busy dealing with him when I visited and could not offer me more time or explanation. I am afraid we will both have to be patient a little longer if we want more information."

"Thank you," I whispered, allowing only one errant tear to slip down my bruised cheek. Swallowing the torrent of sobs that threatened to follow, I managed to find enough of my voice to continue. "I don't like it that everyone around here is being so secretive about his status with me. I keep asking Miriam and Gen, but they brush me off every time. I want you to know that I really do appreciate your being honest with me."

When Ouriel looked as if he'd interrupt me, I stopped him. "No. Seriously. Thank you. I don't know why they think I can't handle what's happening with him. It's harder for me to keep imagining the worst, than it would be for them to just tell me the truth." I rubbed my hands gingerly over eyes that still threatened to flood. "I'm sorry about that." I really had to get myself together. "So—anyway—your visit today—it's about you enrolling at my school? Miriam already told me about that. I don't think it's really going to be necessary. Last night was just some strange mistake. I shouldn't even need protection. There is no reason demons would ever be interested in me. You see, I'm Sightless."

Ouriel, to his credit, did not gasp in dismay at my revelation, nor did he wince. His lack of reaction surprised me. People of Guardian descent were never Sightless.

"Rose, I am well aware of your Sight ability—or apparent lack thereof. However, that does not change the fact that you desperately require protection."

"What?" I asked, dumbfounded.

"Surely you realize those demons were attempting to capture you last night. I saw that clearly for myself."

The idea that he had witnessed the fight humiliated me. I hated that this stranger now knew that I was Sightless *and* that I had no idea how to fight a demon—two mortifying details I'd tried to keep hidden from anyone outside my family.

"You don't understand." I sat up in my bed. "That's not possible! It *must* have been a case of mistaken identity." Did this Warrior really think a group of demons was interested in me? I couldn't see any reason why they would be. None of it made sense. "It's not like they can steal my soul like they can from the Sightless. Thankfully, that's one protection my Guardian blood *did* give me. And I have no power they would be interested in recruiting or torturing me to give my soul for. To demons, I am a nonentity. I may as well not even exist."

Ouriel sighed in exasperation. "Ishmael told me you were stubborn and naïve, but I did not realize to what a great extent. On Friday, just before the attack on Ishmael and yourself, a *coup* of sorts took place in the demon horde, and, it seems, the new leadership *is* interested in you, whether you think that is possible or not. We also have no idea as of yet how this change in power will affect the Endless War, nor do we know who is actually in control on their side. This is a very dangerous time for all of us, *especially* the Sightless. I must not fail in impressing that very important fact upon you."

I was incredulous. "You're serious, right? You really think I'm in danger? Why?"

"That remains for us to determine at a later date. I have my suspicions, but those are not my immediate concern. Your safety, however, is." Ouriel turned to pace the length of my room. "I attempted to persuade Miriam to allow you to remain at home for the near future, but she insists it would be better for you to retain some semblance of routine. Therefore, I have been forced to put into place numerous new procedures for your protection. There will also be stricter constraints on your movement from this moment forward."

"What do you mean?" I asked, not quite sure I wanted to hear the answer.

"You will have to be accompanied by a Warrior whenever you leave this house. As you know, you are perfectly safe here. A demon may not enter a Guardian's home once the proper blessings are put into place. Everywhere else, however, you are extremely vulnerable." Ouriel paused to pierce me with his enigmatic dark blue eyes, probably in an attempt to gauge my reaction to his pronouncement.

"Okay, so I can't go anywhere by myself ever again? Outside of this house?"

"Correct."

Crap. I did *not* want someone tailing me every day. It wasn't as if I went places all that often anyway, but my solitary spirit cringed at the idea of a caretaker and constant companion, especially if it had to be this strange Warrior who already knew way too much about me too soon.

"Seriously?" I tried not to screech, but I could see my life careening out of my control and into the hands of others. "And who is going to be the lucky bodyguard?"

"I am. As you know, I will begin attending your school Monday. I will also escort you at any other time it is necessary for you to go out." Ouriel prowled about my room, looking just as uncomfortable with the idea of following me around as I was to be followed. "From now until you are unequivocally out of danger, you will not leave this house without me in attendance. You are my responsibility."

"*What*? Why are you doing this?" I couldn't believe he had volunteered to babysit me. Who would actually want that kind of "responsibility"? It had to be a step down from his regular duties.

"I owe Ishmael my existence. You are important to him. It was a simple decision to make." The scowl on Ouriel's face belied his true feelings on the subject, and I was beginning to feel hemmed in. The rational part of my mind railed against the idea of spending so much time with this guarded, unapproachable Warrior. I also didn't want to admit, even to myself, that there might be another piece of me that actually wanted him around.

Ouriel cleared his throat. "That leaves us with one last item to discuss—the matter of your education."

"Didn't we just talk about me going back to school?"

Ouriel sighed. "I am not referring to your pursuit of a Sightless High School Diploma. We must discuss your *Guardian* education, which I believe is severely lacking. You have only received the basics, correct?"

"Yeah, I guess. Miriam stopped teaching me when I was about thirteen. That was when we decided I'd start high school. There wasn't much point in going through the rest of the Guardian training when I hadn't shown any signs of the Gift up to that point."

Ouriel studied me for a moment. "Does it bother you, being Sightless?"

His question startled me. No one had ever asked my opinion on the subject before. Most people avoided discussing "my condition" with me in general. I'd always figured it was a concerted effort by my family and their friends to spare my feelings. Ouriel's bluntness should probably have offended me, but I felt only relief. It was refreshing to be asked the question outright, rather than hearing whispers of it behind my back. I found it difficult to answer because I didn't quite know how to explain my feelings.

"It's hard sometimes, especially because I really hate going to a Sightless high school." I shrugged. "I think, though, that I've come to terms with it pretty well." I stopped again, searching for the right words. "I don't think the Gift is something I ever really wanted anyway. Most of my family has died fighting demons. It's ironic that the ability to See is called a gift because it seems to me more like a curse."

"I understand. Losing loved ones in war is never easy. At times, I too feel as though—" Ouriel broke off abruptly. He shifted uneasily, as if he had revealed a bit more of himself than he had meant to. I wanted to force him to finish what he had been going to say, especially because he already knew so many of my secrets. "I am sorry. I have strayed off subject. I had meant to tell you that you will be resuming your Guardian education. You are sorely deficient in both physical and mental training. Sightless or not, you need to be prepared for every eventuality."

I shot Ouriel the cheesiest grin I could muster. "I'm guessing this is not something I can talk you out of?"

He shook his head. I groaned. I really didn't want to go back to learning about demons. Ever. Despite my bravado the night before, I was terrified of them. Just the sight of one made me retch.

"Fine. Just don't let Genevieve teach me. She drives me crazy and gets way too bossy. We haven't been able to get along since her Gift really came in. I don't want Miriam either, much as I love her. She makes me feel bad about myself, just being near her and all her perfection."

Just for a moment, I saw what looked like a smile lurking somewhere in Ouriel's eyes. I wondered briefly if someone besides Ishmael could actually get my sense of humor, but the expression was gone so quickly I wondered if I had imagined it.

Ouriel's face was a hard one to read. "Very well, I will teach you myself, then, seeing as both of your sisters have already declined the post anyway," he replied. "We begin at noon tomorrow."

I was spared the energy of hiding the unexpected pain brought on by the news of my sisters' unwillingness to teach me. Ouriel turned and swept from the room after his final statement. Rendered incapable of thought, I could only bear wordless witness to his abrupt departure from my bedside for the second time in less than twenty-four hours.

∽∾∽

I didn't feel at all rested when noon on Sunday arrived. My mind was still spinning from the painkillers and muscle relaxants I'd had to take just to sleep when I heard Miriam let Ouriel in. Desperate, I tried to do something with my wretched hair, but my broken ribs restricted any movement to futile attempts. I brushed my bangs across my forehead again, trying to cover my stitches and not flinch from the agony, but they kept falling forward into my eyes. *A meeting with Ouriel is not worth all this trouble*, I scolded myself, surprised to find that I actually meant it.

I gave up and shoved my hair into a low ponytail. I'd never cared if boys noticed me before, and I wasn't going to start with this one, no matter how great the temptation.

Besides, I had much more important things to freak out about.

I left my room and walked quietly toward the kitchen. From the intensity of their whispered voices, I could tell Ouriel and Miriam were locked in a heated debate. I ducked back behind the wall and listened to their conversation.

"You have allowed her to carry on like this far too long." He sounded aggravated.

"You don't know how often I wanted to tell her, Ouriel, but I just couldn't. You are seeing her as the rebellious teenager she is now. Remember her as the scared little girl you first saw thirteen years ago—you would have made the same decisions!"

What? Ouriel had seen me as child? I supposed that wasn't too crazy a possibility. *Surely he had been to my parents' funeral. But had I known him at all?* Before I could continue the thought, Ouriel's next statement wrecked that train and sent me spinning in a different direction.

"Be that as it may, she will learn the truth sometime. She is stronger than you believe. You should never have ended her training."

My mind fishtailed out of control.

"I was doing the best I could! She was so fragile, almost to her breaking point, and I didn't want to overwhelm her—"

"Stop. She is listening. Show yourself, Rose."

I slunk around the corner and jumped on the offensive to cover my guilt. "What aren't you guys telling me?

And don't say you weren't just talking about me! I heard enough to know that you were."

Ouriel looked to Miriam, allowing her to take the lead. "Rose, honey, we weren't talking about anything important. We're just worried about you. We need to find out why you might be in danger. The idea that demons would want to kidnap you doesn't make any sense."

Ouriel blew out a quick breath and slanted an aggrieved look at Miriam, so I grilled him, "Is that true, Ouriel? You have no idea why they would want me either?"

"I have no reason that I can tell you at the moment." Ouriel bit out each word. Before I could figure out whether he was angry with Miriam or me, he charged on, "If you will excuse us, Miriam, Rose and I have work to do. Come, Rose, let us sit on your back porch and review what little knowledge you have of the Endless War."

Uneasy, I led the Warrior out of the kitchen, down a long hall, and through the backdoor. Our old, historic home rambled with too much space for the few members who remained of my once-large family, but the backyard promised cool serenity for any of us trying to escape the emptiness. Seeking that peace, I continued out onto the grass, while Ouriel remained on the patio.

The garden was beautiful this time of year. Late summer rains had turned the lawn a deep, dark green, and the flowerbeds burst with color. Miriam put a lot of effort and her free time into all of it. She adored her masses of light blue plumbago and tall bushes of fuchsia bougainvillea. Surrounded by all that beauty, I turned my face to the sun, lapping up every bit of warmth and strength it had to offer.

It *was* peaceful in the yard, but the August sun beat down on me, relentless and scorching. I began to sweat. I returned to the coolness of the porch, where Ouriel had been waiting and watching me with his typical inscrutable expression. Careful of my injuries, I lowered myself gingerly onto the soft cushion of a lawn chair and sighed. Ouriel took the chair across from me.

"Any news on Ish?" I needed to know his condition before beginning anything else.

"No, I am sorry to say. He remains the same as I reported to you yesterday. I will, however, endeavor to learn more for you this evening."

"Thank you." I shook off a sudden attack of melancholy before Ouriel could catch scent of it. "So, what do we do now?"

"First, I must conduct an oral assessment of how much you know, so that I may determine where the gaps in your knowledge exist. In this way, I will be able to better devise a plan for teaching you. I will ask you a series of the most basic questions. This is not to insult you, but rather to clarify how we should proceed in regards to your instruction. Are you ready?" I nodded. "Very well. How did the Endless War begin?"

"Well…" My hands went numb with anxiety. "Even the Sightless know the beginning. They've gotten it confused after millennia of oral tradition, but the basic story remains the same. After He had fashioned the angels and the universe, God, or Elohim as we Guardians refer to

IIim, created humans. When He hailed us as His greatest creation, Lucifer, or Helel as he is actually called, grew jealous of the inferior humans and turned against God. Michael, God's beloved, then forced Helel out of Heaven. In the Fall, Helel and his followers became twisted with evil and hatred. They transformed into demons. Since that time, they have walked the earth devouring human souls and tempting the most powerful to come to their side and betray the Creator…" I trailed off, not knowing what he wanted to hear next.

"How did Guardians come into being?" Ouriel prompted.

"We are the descendants of Esau, twin brother of Jacob, son of Isaac, grandson of Abraham. We were beloved by God for many centuries, although He did not guard us as jealously as He did the Israelites. I don't know why. Maybe He hoped we'd all eventually reconnect as one big, happy family or something. He even ordered them to keep peace with us, their 'brothers,' after their escape from Egypt. But it never happened. Or maybe this was all part of His grand plan. Who knows?" I shook my head. "Eventually, Helel tempted many of my ancestors into evil. The few of us who remained faithful to Elohim were blessed—as well as cursed for our fathers' betrayals—with protecting the rest of His precious creations. We were said to have been wiped from the face of the earth. And we did disappear from normal human life and have lived separately ever since.

"However, we were given powers beyond the ordinary human in order to fight the Fallen. We were granted the ability to See, although for each of us, the Gift is different and unique. We're still much more fragile than Warriors, but, unlike other humans, demons cannot take our souls without our consent. Likewise, we cannot kill them. We can fight to prevent demons from attacking a defenseless human and damage them in any way possible, but only fire conjured by a Warrior can truly end a demon's existence. Like all angels and Warriors, however, if we willingly betray God, we too will become demons ourselves."

"Do you know the differences between Guardians, Warriors, and angels?"

"Yes," I scoffed, a little insulted, despite his earlier disclaimer. Even if Ouriel had to scrutinize my understanding of the fundamentals, it seemed to me that this question took it a bit too far. "Guardians are human. Warriors and angels are not. In fact, Warriors are a special case unto themselves. You began as an order of angels, but have since evolved into something different, like a hybrid between humanity and the angelic because of your class's constant contact with death and war."

"Good. Now, describe the variations of the Gift which exist in your family."

This was a little more difficult for me to explain. The ability to See was ephemeral, at best. It was always unique to each Guardian—even to each Warrior, although their abilities were more concentrated in general.

"Um…okay…let's start with Miriam. She has Foresight, to an extent, and the ability to See that which she needs to know to survive. When this particular Gift is given, the divine communication usually comes in the form of dreams, but she can also have visions when the need arises.

"Shadrach is kind of like a one way radio receiver. He can pick up the thoughts and intentions of others, even if you don't want him to. A person can send him specific messages from great distances. The problem is, he can't send any back, of course, unless the other person is a receiver as well. The limits of that part of his Gift can be really frustrating at times. He can also do a little mind-bending, as I like to call it." I giggled at my own quip. *Yikes! How dorky could I be?* "Uh...anyway, weak mind-ed people are often susceptible to his powers of sugges-tion.

"Genevieve's Gift is much more difficult to explain than the others'. It's hard for anyone, even her, to under-stand sometimes. She communicates with spirits. It is of-ten said that God only entrusts a very few people with this particular type of Sight because so few can control it, and some may find it too tempting to use their Gift for evil. Not only does she gain information from the spirits, but she also helps them. That part of her thing is almost like that TV show, you know?"

Ouriel stared at me blankly in response. *Could I not stop with the pop culture references?*

"You know, Jennifer Whateverhernameis? Her char-acter sees 'earthbound spirits' and helps them find the light? Cross over into Heaven or whatever?"

Still nothing. Just silence.

"Well, Genevieve does kind of the same thing and tries to help all the spirits she sees to find true happiness and peace with God. Meanwhile, they do what they can to help Gen protect humans.

"My mother was a Healer, as in the 'Laying of Hands' type, and my father had some of Miriam's Gift and telekinesis type stuff." I paused to catch my breath after the long speech.

"Very good. I am impressed with your basic knowledge." Ouriel twisted his face into what he must have thought passed for a smile. "Do you know your ancestral litany?"

"Must I recite the entire lineage?" I rolled my eyes. "Look, it starts with a woman named Verdah on my mom's side and ends with me, okay? Do I really have to name everyone else? The whole thing wears me out. And to tell you the truth, I don't enjoy it much. Instead, can it just suffice for me to say that my clan lived among the Canaanites in more ancient times, converted to Christianity in the time of Christ, was later instrumental in building the Maronite branch of the Catholic Church, and emigrated to the United States only by accident in the early 1900s because of the outbreak of World War I?"

"That will certainly suffice," the Warrior sniffed. "I also do not care to recount my ancestry. Although, thanks to the long lives of Warriors, mine is much shorter than yours. I am only two generations removed from the original Creation."

That tiny bit of information from Ouriel titillated me. "Really? How old are you then? I know that Ishmael is second generation, and he was born somewhere around the time of Noah." Probably because I'd never been able to pry much out of Ish on the subject of his relatives, the family histories of Warriors interested me much more than my own.

"I am young in terms of Warriors. I came into being after the time of the Christ."

"Really? I'd love to have seen all the history you have! What's been your favorite time period?" I leaned toward him and, in my enthusiasm, touched the back of Ouriel's hand. He snatched it away, his expression hardened, and the emotion in his eyes went flat.

"We are off subject and must regain focus," he snapped.

Why was it, every time he shared even the tiniest bit of himself with me, Ouriel seemed to regret it and close himself off? All while requiring me to express in detail parts of myself I preferred remain neglected? I wanted to rant at the injustice, but his quick redirection threw me off.

"Your basic knowledge is solid," he intoned, oblivious to my aggravation. "However, I am impatient to begin your physical training. It is unfortunate that we must wait until your ribs and head have healed. When that time comes, we must also deal with the business of selecting a weapon for you, teaching you how to protect a human under attack, and some rudimentary self-protection."

"Why? I don't need to know those things. I can't See. I'll never be able to fight!"

Ouriel arched his brows at me. "That may be the case, but I am determined that you will know how to protect yourself and others, if the need arises. Your family has done you a serious disservice in not having done so years ago. It does not matter if you plan to engage a demon or not. You are of Guardian blood. The time will come when you must protect yourself because no one will be near enough to help you. You must be prepared."

"You're serious, aren't you? You really believe that someone's after me? That I might have to fight demons?" Fear rustled in the pit of my stomach. However I might have felt about being Sightless, I'd never wanted to fight demons. They petrified me. My nightmares had ensured that—as had the loss of nearly everyone I'd ever loved to the War. I clamped my arms around my midsection to stave off the wave of nausea I knew was coming.

"Have I frightened you?" Ouriel murmured.

I nodded.

"Good. Then our lesson today has been a success. You must understand the very real danger that permeates your existence. The next time you confront a demon as you did Friday night, I am determined that you will be ready for the fight."

I gaped at Ouriel. He seemed to be gloating over the terror I was experiencing, and my palms itched to smack the smug look off his face. The thought of his reaction to *that* made me feel slightly better, until I remembered his mention of the "next" time I fought a demon. The thought chased the laughter right back down my constricted throat.

The next time I fought a demon? I couldn't believe there'd even been a first time!

What had happened to my peaceful life?

"Well, I believe we have done enough for today, especially considering your weakened condition." Ouriel stood and prepared to leave. "I will be here to escort you to school in the morning. You will be ready no later than 7:30."

I remained sitting, only to be forced to look up at him towering over me. I couldn't imagine this aloof Warrior passing for a normal human teenager. I also didn't know whether to groan or laugh at the thought of him trying.

"I'll be ready. How are we getting there? The truck? Shouldn't we show up separately? And what's our cover story? Am I even supposed to know you?" It had struck me that many of the details had yet to be worked out.

"I will be Jumping you to school from now on. I have prepared a location there for expressly that purpose," Ouriel replied. "We will enter the building separately. I am also placing Warriors all around your school as a precaution. We will not be ambushed there again. It is my goal that your school be as safe as it possibly can be. As for our…er…cover story, as you termed it, I believe we will pretend not to know each other. That should be much easier than creating an elaborate pretense of some sort." Ouriel hesitated. "Rose, are you all right? You don't look well."

I guessed that my face had become very pale, since I'd felt all the blood drain out of my head. My brain had frozen at the idea of Jumping to school with Ouriel. I wasn't sure I wanted to be as close to him as that would require. My insides numbed disturbingly at the thought. In fact, I was pretty sure my face had just flicked from white to flaming red when I imagined Ouriel wrapping his amber arms around me.

No male, outside my family, had ever touched me so intimately in all of my short life.

"Rose?" Ouriel asked again, real worry creeping into his voice.

I gave myself a mental headshake and forced my errant mind to function. "I'm…uh…I'm fine! I was—" I paused. I really needed to lie here, but I didn't know if Ouriel possessed the power to divine the truth. I sucked in a deep breath and went for it. "I was just freaking out some more about that whole fighting demons stuff. It really scares me."

Ouriel studied me as I spoke. His expression didn't change until he finally nodded, seeming pleased with himself. "I am glad you now understand the gravity of your situation. However, you need not worry too much. As I stated earlier, I will ensure that you are able to defend yourself better the next time you are required to fight." He grabbed the sword that never seemed to be very far out of his reach off a nearby table.

I couldn't tell for sure, but I was pretty positive that Ouriel hadn't recognized my fib.

That was good.

No, it was better than good. Ouriel couldn't sense lies! I smiled at that little fact, as it might allow me to keep at least some of my innermost thoughts private for the next few weeks.

I guided Ouriel around the outside of my house to the towering front gate. Slinging his sword in its scabbard over his head and one shoulder, Ouriel bowed stiffly. "Goodbye, Rose. I will see you in the morning."

Not knowing what else to do, I bowed slightly in return, trying not to hurt myself, and before I could reach to open the gate for him, Ouriel melted away. *Guess I can see why my grandparents put in a ten foot fence covered with ivy a hundred years ago. Comes in handy for all the weirdoes popping in and out of here day and night.*

I went to bed that night, and, instead of my regular nightmare, I dreamed of nothingness.

CHAPTER 3

For the first time in longer than I could remember, I slept without waking. It was an immense relief to not be subjected to watching a continuous loop of my nightmare, and I woke feeling rested. As a result, I was actually ready when Ouriel Jumped into our front hallway.

I tried not to notice how good he looked in his uniform white button down shirt and tie but quickly gave it up as pointless. Ouriel wore navy blue Dockers, black dress shoes, and his hair pulled back into a ponytail that sat at the nape of his neck. Only the sword that never seemed to leave his back ruined the perfect Catholic schoolboy image.

"You're not going to be walking down the halls with that thing strapped to your back are you?" I pointed to his blade with what was probably a sappy grin on my face.

"It might be a dead giveaway that you're not who you say you are."

Ouriel shocked me into silence when he turned to smirk back at me. "Despite appearances, I actually have some knowledge of Sightless customs and fashion."

I wondered what had put him in such a lighthearted mood. *Maybe he's just a morning person?*

"In fact, I have brought this along to keep in its stead while inside your school." Ouriel's eyes glowed with boyish anticipation as he produced a backpack. He unzipped it and pulled a huge knife out from in between tons of brand new notebooks. When he held it out reverently for my inspection, I saw that the blade was at least ten inches long.

"Holy crap, Ouriel!" I shrieked. "What is that?"

"Is it not extraordinary…er…cool?" he gushed. "It is a coffin handled Bowie knife. I can conceal it in this contrivance you humans use to carry your supplies."

Heaven help me! He does have some emotions behind that distant exterior. Too bad they happened to be so geeky. I shook my head. "The contrivance is called a backpack, and it's not for carrying weapons. In fact, they are highly illegal in schools. You're going to have to keep that very well hidden or you may end up in jail, no matter how good a reason you have for carrying it around. I'd love to see you talk your way out of that!"

I couldn't smother a small laugh, and I paid dearly for it with rib pain, which was compounded by the fact that Ouriel didn't find my humor very funny. He seemed personally affronted that his dangerous toy hadn't impressed me.

"I would not expect you to understand the bond between a Warrior and his blade, as sorely lacking as your education has been."

Chastened, I tried to make amends for my perceived mockery. "I'm sorry, Ouriel. It is a cool knife. And I am really glad you're here to protect me with it." He didn't respond, and we fell into an uncomfortable silence. I scrambled for something to say and came up with a truly brilliant comment. "Well…uh…I guess we had better get going. How many Jumps do you think we're going to have to make?"

Ouriel shot me a smug look. "Only one. I am a superior Jumper."

"Okay, then." I faltered again. "So—where will we be Jumping to exactly? And—um—how do you prefer to—to—do it?" I finished lamely. My palms began to sweat and the bottom dropped out of my stomach. *Could I be a bigger idiot? Agh*! I sounded like a virgin Jumper who could barely speak her own language.

Ouriel's initial response to my question consisted of a strange look, followed by some kind of emotion that burned in his eyes before being shuttered by his usual impenetrable mask.

"We will be Jumping onto the Convent grounds adjacent to the gymnasium," he answered smoothly. "There is a shed just outside the nuns' garden that is backed up to within two feet of the bordering rock wall, creating a sheltered area into which we may arrive unseen. We can leave the spot separately and walk into the school. You are to say Miriam has dropped you off. She has already informed the principal that you and Ishmael were involved in a serious car accident and he will not return to work for an uncertain amount of time."

I noticed he hadn't mentioned exactly how we were going to Jump in his little speech. Had I offended him with my bumbled question about how we were going to "do it"? Eaten up with insecurity and embarrassment, I started to apologize when I was interrupted by Miriam and Genevieve stumbling past us on their way to the kitchen. Both still wore their pajamas after a long night on duty.

"Oh, Ouri! Good morning," Miriam yawned.

Gen smirked at me. "I can't believe you're actually ready. It's a miracle! I don't know what magic you've worked on her Ouri, but Ish was never able to scare her into being ready this early in the morning."

"Shut up, Genevieve," I grumbled after her.

"That isn't polite, Rose," Gen drawled from somewhere in the other room. "You shouldn't talk to your sister like that in front of Ouriel! You wouldn't want him to know what a brat you are so soon, would you?"

She surprised a creaky bark of laughter out of Ouriel, and the sound of it grated on my already overwrought nerves. It was my turn to glare at him.

"Ahem." Ouriel cleared his throat and had the decency to look abashed. "We must be leaving now. To use your words, how would you—uh—prefer to do it?" Ouriel asked with a hint of sarcasm.

"I don't know. My sisters have never Jumped me farther than the basement, and they only needed to hold my hand for that. Ish always held me in his arms, but he's been Jumping me places since I was four, so that was just kind of a habit. I wouldn't know what else to do…"

"Well, I have never Jumped with another being, but I know the bond must be secure for a Jump of this distance." Ouriel's brow furrowed. "I do not believe holding hands will suffice, so—I suppose we must—embrace." Ouriel choked on that last word. He seemed unnerved by the thought of touching me but proceeded to reach for me anyway, resigned.

Following his lead, I submitted to the situation with as much grace as I could muster. I grabbed my backpack, put it on, and stepped toward him. By unspoken agreement, we looked anywhere but at each other as he put his arms around me. I wrapped mine tightly around his waist.

Risking a cursory glance, I saw that he remained unreadable, as always, but I was unable to hide my tormented emotions. Everything felt wrong about touching Ouriel. Just being near him made me miss Ishmael. Desperate to hide an onslaught of tears, I rested my cheek as lightly as possible on Ouriel's chest. Our bodies melted into nothingness.

We reappeared exactly where he had said we would—crammed between the caretaker's shed and the rock wall. I was breathless. His body felt solid and strong pressed so close to mine. I didn't want to let go, but I noticed that Ouriel had gone deathly still.

"Are you all right?" I asked, stepping back.

Struggling to control his breathing, Ouriel finally gasped, "I am fine. That was a new experience for me, but do not fret. I will soon grow accustomed to Jumping with you."

I hoped I could do the same.

ɔɛɔ

Ouriel insisted that I make the trek across the black-top playground to the school building first, in order to keep watch on me. When I reached for the powder blue door, an older man burst through it and snapped me up into crushing hug that almost caused me to black out in pain.

"*¡Rosa, mija! ¿Estás bien? Déjame ver,*" the man cried and proceeded to hold me up for inspection.

Javier, my attacker, served as the caretaker cum gardener that had worked for the nuns who ran Father Yermo for as long as anyone could remember. He was one of the few people I considered a friend—or what passed as a friend in my life—seeing as he was the only person besides Ish that I willingly spoke to at school. Rather than feeling any self-pity for my lack of conventional friends, his agony-inducing concern pleased me. Javier's familiar face creased like the brown of a used paper sack as he frowned at my beat up face and clucked his dismay.

"I'm okay, Javi, really. Considering everything, you know…"

"*Sí, mija.* I know about your accident. And how is your father, Ishmael?"

"He's not doing very well. We don't have much information right now, but I think he'll be okay. Eventually."

"*Ay,* Rosa, if there is anything I can do, please tell me. Your father, he is a good man. He always helps me when he can. Yes, he is a very good man, and you are a very good daughter to him. You will tell me if I can help you, *no*?"

"Yes, Javier," I said, embarrassed by the kindness he was showing me. I ducked my head and hurried around him and into the building before he could see the tears welling up in my eyes. Before I got too far, I remembered my manners and managed to call back to him, "Oh, and Javier—thank you!"

I couldn't hear his response over my sobs. I had to run, as best as I could, for the bathroom before I totally humiliated myself. Luckily, it was empty so no one else witnessed my mini-breakdown. After a few minutes of alternating between silent sniveling and the pain sobbing induced in my ribs, I got myself together enough to head for my locker. I walked through the quickly filling hall to my assigned spot. Dialing the combination to yank my lock open, I realized I'd been too preoccupied to see whether or not Ouriel had actually followed me into the building.

And I didn't know if he had until he walked into my first period class, only a minute before the tardy bell. Mrs. Palmer had just finished asking me about Ishmael when Ouriel sauntered in. She met him at the front of the class, and he handed her his schedule.

"Ouriel San Miguel?" Her tongue tripped over his name. "Did I say that right?"

"No ma'am. It is more like the 'oo' sound in soon. *Oo-ree-el*, not *oh-ree-ole*, like the bird."

Mrs. Palmer repeated after him, "Oooo-ree-el. Got it. Sorry about that. I've never been good with names. Let's see…" She paused to look around the classroom. "You can sit over there in the empty seat behind Rose. Rose, sweetie, can you raise your hand please?"

I smothered a groan as I put my hand in the air. Ouriel didn't look too pleased about sitting so close to me either. He walked toward me, and every girl in the room devoured him with her eyes. I felt a strange possessive urge to slap each of them until he passed by me and whispered, "This gives new meaning to the human saying, 'watching your back.'" Then he said to me more publicly, "Hello. I am Ouriel. Nice to meet you."

I turned in my seat and shook the hand he offered. "I'm Rose Kazin. Nice to meet you, too, Ouriel."

I embarrassed myself by giggling like the schoolgirl I didn't want to be. *Holy crap! I'm turning into an emotional freak.* Even worse, the noise caused every girl in the room to tear her gaze from Ouriel to focus on me. My inane laughter died out when I felt the nasty weight of so many eyes slamming into me. I really hated being noticed by the other girls in my class.

And, now, each of them was staring daggers at me.

Well, all of them except one. A quiet girl named Taylor Gomez was looking at me with a conspiratorial gleam in her eyes. I wondered what that meant but didn't

have time to consider it too much before the bell rang.
With the ease that comes of years of practice, the entire
class stood up as one for the national anthem. When it
finished, I grinned to myself as Ouriel crossed himself for
the beginning of the morning prayer. I tried to imagine
what those girls' reactions would be if I told them they
were praying with an actual Warrior—as if they would
even know what that meant.

After the announcements, the rest of my morning
passed in a haze of classes, each of them containing the
new student everyone couldn't stop talking about. No
matter how many girls attempted to engage him in conversation, Ouriel remained oblivious to all the attention.
But he never took his eyes off me—a fact many of the
girls noticed. They spent all morning speculating on why
the "hot new boy" would be so interested in me, a total
social outsider. It gave me no satisfaction to know the
true answer. It was much less glamorous than they could
have guessed.

I walked to lunch dreading the fact that Ouriel was
going to see me eating alone and know just how sad my
high school existence really was. I claimed my tray of
food and sat in my usual spot. Ouriel surprised me by
joining me with his tray.

I imagined how sad and lonely I must look to him.
Just thinking about the idea that he found me pitiable
made me want to bang my head on the table. Instead, I
remembered I was pretty much a loner by choice and
drew together what remained of my pride from somewhere deep in my soul.

"You don't have to sit with me, Ouriel. I'm sure just about any person here would want you to sit by them today, even the guys."

"I have no wish to sit elsewhere."

"Really?" I tried not to sound surprised.

"Really."

I tried to determine whether or not his voice held the hint of a smile as a tall, thin girl approached us. I winced. Ana Ruiz was *not* a nice person. With long, wavy, dark hair and golden brown skin, she looked like a South American model. I cringed and wanted to sink into the floor before she got to us, but there was no escape for me.

As if she hadn't been planning it since first seeing me beat up that morning, Ana said, "Oh my God, Rose, what happened to your face?"

I did my best to conceal my disgust for her. "I was in a car accident."

"Oh, that's too bad," she pouted. "I'm glad you're all right, but it *is* awful about that horrible cut on your face. It looks like it'll leave an ugly scar." She shook her head in mock concern, turned her malicious olive green eyes to Ouriel, and smiled. "Hi! I'm Ana Ruiz. I saw you this morning in first period. My friends and I usually sit over there for lunch if you ever want to join us. I'm hoping I get to see more of you now that you know me. And not just in first period, either!" Ana tossed her gorgeous, well-groomed hair with a giggle and, to my great relief, walked away without another word.

Left with an uncomfortable silence, my nerves kicked in. Trying to cover them, I blurted out the first trivial fact to enter my mind. "Gen's real name isn't actually Genevieve!"

Ouriel paused in midbite of his *flauta*. "What?"

His offhanded question encouraged my mouth to take on a life of its own, as it often does when I'm anxious. "Yeah, her first name is the Arabic *Jamale*, but she hates it because nobody around here can pronounce it right, so she goes by her middle name." Couldn't I just shut up already? "See, Spanish speakers tend to say *Ha-mah-leh* and the American accent is even worse, *Ja-mah-lee*. Isn't that awful?"

I giggled, still trying to shut myself up, but the blabbering continued unabated. "It's actually pronounced '*Zhe-mee-leh*' and Gen got so tired of correcting people that she just gave up. Her actual name is Jamale Genevieve Al'Khazzen. Of course, the Genevieve part is pronounced with the French accent. Because, you know, we Lebanese love our Arabic and French. Did you know we intermarried with many of the French Crusaders early in the last millennium? That explains my blonde hair, right? Of course, I don't speak Arabic. Or French. *Sitte* Rosie, my grandmother, she said we didn't need to learn those languages, living here on the Mexican border, so she taught us Spanish instead. Ironic considering the state of the Middle East these days, huh? By the way, my real name is pronounced *Rou-sah*, with the 'ou' sound like in 'ouch.' Only Ishmael ever uses the original pronunciation." My words dried up and left me deflated and embarrassed. "You probably already knew all that, didn't you?"

Clearly perplexed, Ouriel managed to nod in response.

Sensing that I may have finally run out of blathering, I ducked my head and shoved a *flauta* into my mouth to make sure I couldn't open it again. We spent the rest of the lunch period in silence, uninterrupted by my idiotic mania.

❧❧❧

The rest of our school day passed uneventfully. It felt strange to walk out of the school building right after the bell rang. Doing so without Ishmael disconcerted me even more. As I limped across the playground toward my meeting place with Ouriel, I glanced at the spot where I had last seen Ishmael whole and healthy, ready to defend me to the death. I cringed at the picture that painted itself in my mind of what Ishmael must have looked like after the attack—his beautiful amber body broken and mangled, his bright red blood spilling onto the sizzling black asphalt beneath him.

It killed me, not knowing the extent of his injuries or when he might be well again. Because he was nearly immortal, the idea that Ishmael could die had never entered my mind before our attack. Thinking about what my life would be like without him was painful. I fought back the panic, despite my racing heart and pounding head.

Very slowly, I crossed the playground near the gym and turned the corner toward the shed. I looked only once over my shoulder—to see if Ouriel was having difficulty following my torturous progress. I needn't have worried. He was about fifty meters behind me, strolling along, appearing to study the surroundings of his new school. But I knew that he was alert and could close the distance between us in a split second if he had to.

I checked my surroundings once more to make sure that no one saw me as I ducked behind the shed. Ouriel arrived a few moments later. He pulled his sword out from underneath the shed—where he must have hidden it that morning—and buckled it on. He looked at me, hesitant to bring our bodies closer together. I could tell that he didn't want to be anywhere near enough to me to Jump us home. With my emotions already in flux over Ishmael, I didn't want Ouriel touching me either.

Resolved to the inevitable, we stepped together and wrapped our arms around one another. Ouriel's scent registered in my brain. The combination felt intoxicating.

We landed silently in my front hall, gasping for breath. We tore our bodies apart, and I grabbed the nearest object, a giant concrete statue of the Virgin Mary, for balance. I jerked back only to knock into Ouriel. He had been leaning against the wall where the hall and foyer came together, and my surprise attack plunged him headfirst into the sharp corner.

My ribs screeched in protest and the gash in my head throbbed. "Oh, crap! I'm so sorry!"

He said nothing and only looked at the dent his head had left in what had been two perpendicular walls coming together in a crisp right angle.

"Ouriel, are you okay?" I asked, frantic that I might have already broken my *replacement* bodyguard.

"Yes. I am fine. Your wall, on the other hand, is definitely the worse for wear."

"Yeah. And now Miriam's gonna kill me."

"I doubt that. She may be sorely tempted, however." Ouriel shook his head. "Tell me, are you often prone to accidents of this nature?"

"No!" I snapped, stung by the sarcasm in his words. "Usually, I'm very coordinated. I'm just a little out of it since…well…since Ish." I shivered with the pain of saying his name aloud.

"Rose, are you all right? I had thought there was no major damage done to you in our little collision—"

"I'm fine!"

"Are you sure? I felt at first that you had only jarred yourself a bit, but your wince just then—it carried with it a great deal of pain. Are my senses off?"

"Your stupid senses are not off. I didn't damage myself permanently or anything," I ground out, crushing myself with a hug to hold my ribs in place. "I just miss Ish!"

"Oh." Ouriel looked distinctly uncomfortable. "You must be worried about him."

"Hello! Of course I am!" *Crap.* Yelling hurt. Now I felt like the stupid one. "Have you heard anything else about his condition yet?"

"Only one small fact, Rose. I am sorry I did not disclose it to you earlier today, but I was loath to further agitate you. I was informed late last night that he has been taken into celestial care."

"Celestial care?" I'd never heard the term, which wasn't all that surprising considering the fact that I knew very few Warriors.

"Yes. His injuries were so extensive that he has been returned to the celestial realm temporarily. Our healers were unable to deal with him here. One might say that he has been placed in the angelic form of a Critical Care Unit."

"He's that bad, then?" I'd almost kept the quiver out of my voice.

Ouriel frowned. "He is indeed. His situation worsened last night with what seemed like an aggressive infection growing in a large gash on his leg."

"So now there's no way I can see him, huh?"

"No. Again, I am sorry." He studied me. "You care for him a great deal, do you not?"

"Of course I do!" Did he have to grapple with every simple emotion? "He's helped to raise me as if I was his own since my parents died."

Ouriel nodded. "He is a great Warrior." To his credit, he hesitated for only a second before patting my shoulder awkwardly. "But enough of that. Come, we need to continue your training. As you are not in any condition to do physical work, we will delve into more Guardian history."

I gaped at Ouriel's back as he turned and walked away. He sensed that I was in a torment of pain over Ishmael but had absolutely no idea what to do about it. I shook my head and realized that the guy must be more emotionally stunted than I'd thought. *Yikes*!

All I got was "He's a great Warrior" and a pat on the back for my pain?

Stifling an exasperated half-sob/half-giggle, I followed Ouriel down the hall toward our kitchen. I sat, rather painfully, in one of the oak chairs directly across the table from him. I tried to make myself comfortable in a chair whose latticework back left much to be desired for ribs sore from a long, stressful day.

"So, what's up for tonight?"

"Yesterday we discussed your family lineage sparingly and chose to forego the monotony of listing each of your predecessors. That was well enough for a beginning, but today I would like to review your family in greater detail." Ouriel stopped short at my loud snort and flashed what I recognized as his usual almost-but-not-quite smile. "Do not concern yourself too much, Rose. We will restrict ourselves to only discussing the better known of your ancestors."

His words struck a deep chord within me, and my body went instantly rigid. My mind launched back to a time where a much younger me sat at the knee of my mother's mother to first hear the long heralded stories of my family. A great sadness drenched me. I could see two women, both long gone, perfectly—my tiny, dark grandmother, sitting with her ankles tucked beneath her, and my gorgeous mother, laughing just beyond her.

And their voices. *God help me*! I heard their sweet voices ringing in my head as they regaled me with the loose threads of memory that bound up the fabric of our ancestral history.

'*You come from a long line of powerful Guardians, Rousa. Remember that. We have been at war with evil for thousands of years. And you will carry on that tradition. You are descended from greatness, tempered in equal amounts by suffering, darling—each bestowed upon us by God Himself. Never cease to be proud of those who came before you. We will be a comfort to you later in the darkest hours of your life…*'

For only a second, their voices mixed with Ouriel's, as he called me back to the present. "*Rousa*—Rose, are you all right?"

"What?" Disoriented, it took me a moment to fight down the yearning that overwhelmed me in reliving just those few, glorious moments with my mother and grandmother. I reached a shaky hand up to my unfocused eyes, only to find they were wet. I shot up to get away from Ouriel before he could see I was crying. My ribs and head throbbed so loudly I had to grab for the back of my chair or pass out.

"*Rose?*" Ouriel shifted into full paranoid mode. "Where are you in pain? I can feel it, but I cannot tell from which injury it is coming."

I resisted the urge to bark rudely back. "That's because it's an old injury. And it's not a physical one."

"Oh." Ouriel slowly, very slowly, reached out and pried my fingers from the back of the kitchen chair.

Shocked by the extraordinary warmth of his skin, I realized that he had never before touched my bare skin.

His hands shook, but he gently maneuvered me back into the chair. He paled, and his breathing became labored.

"Ouriel, what's wrong? Are you okay? Your hand, it was so warm."

"I am fine. All Warriors give off great amounts of heat—"

"I know that! I hold Ish's hand all the time. But *your* heat…I don't know how to explain it!" Frustrated, I tried again. "Your warmth, it's not that it's any hotter than Ishmael's, it's just more…intense or something."

"Yes, it is." Ouriel turned away from me.

"Well?"

He rounded on me, and blue fire blazed in his eyes. "Well, what?

"Well, I—I was just wondering why—"

"And if I do not wish to tell you?"

"Then you don't have to," I whispered.

I watched as he seemed to wage a sort of battle in his mind. The flames that had jumped from his eyes to flicker down his arms receded, and his breathing slowed. His coloring, which had been so pale, burned bronze.

"Rose, I am sorry," he panted. "Please forgive me. I did not mean to snap at you. You see, the intense feeling of my skin is part of my Gift. It is a gift, which, as you pointed out so brilliantly yesterday, can also be a great burden."

"What do you mean? Uh…only if you want to tell me…" Why didn't I know when to shut up?

Ouriel's shout of laughter—a creaking sound that reeked of non-use—dispelled any further tension in the room. "Do not worry, Rose. I will not yell at you again tonight. I have myself under control now. You see, one of my Gifts is the ability to heal others. I can feel a person's pain resonating and amplified, if you will, in my own body. Had I chosen to be a Healer, I could use that power to seek out the illnesses or injuries of others. When I touch someone, my skin picks up on his or her wellbeing, both physical and mental. My mind instantly perceives exactly that which pains, or soothes, as it were."

"And this is only when you touch someone?"

"Yes and no. I can feel the ambient emotions of the people around me, but it is a skill more ephemeral in nature. It is more difficult for me to decipher feelings that way, partly because skin to skin contact heightens the connection, but also because I have chosen not to hone my ability."

"And you've chosen not to use this Gift of yours because…"

Ouriel shot a real grin at me. "Not bashful for long are you?"

"Nosiness is one of my more obvious—and less attractive—traits." I shrugged. "Sorry."

"Do not apologize, my little *pepa*. As far as your many flaws are concerned, it ranks as only a minor one."

My mouth dropped open. "Ouriel, did you just make a joke?"

He looked disappointed. "Yes, although it must not have been very humorous. You did not laugh."

"That's only because I'm so shocked." Now, I struggled not to laugh at *him* when his face twisted into a skeptical glare. I couldn't fall out of my chair guffaw-ing—it would be too painful—so I settled for a little snort instead.

And to my surprise, Ouriel didn't react with injured pride.

Instead, a small miracle occurred, and he laughed with me.

CHAPTER 4

Tell me," Ouriel wheezed when our laughter died out. "What do you know of your family?"

"Well, I know that, on my mom's side, we are one of the oldest Guardian bloodlines. Her side of the family is still very much focused in the Holy Land. We're one of the few cadet branches that haven't returned there after a few generations. It's the same way with my father's line, well, except for his offshoot that ended up in Ireland—most of which is still there today. I also know that we have produced the greatest female Guardians in history. And, although some are still quite famous today, we've never been discovered—even though we came really close with Joan of Arc."

"True. I remember that well. It was a sad, sad time for your family. I had not yet begun to fight, but I remember how greatly admired she was. Tell me more."

"Okay, but I need a glass of water first." I got up slowly, rounded the counter, and headed for the sink. "Would you like one?"

"Yes, please."

I reached for two glasses in the upper cabinet and winced as the twinge in my ribs shot throughout my body. "Ow! Crap. All right, so Joan of Arc was the most recent of my family to have had a huge impact on world events. She wasn't really French, of course, but came from my family's stronghold in the Near East. One of her Gifts was for language and she integrated easily into the peasantry of France."

"How are you related?" Ouriel asked as water from the refrigerator spigot splashed into the second cup.

"She is my great-grandmother, of some sort." I sat back down and handed him his glass. "While she was still rather young—even though she had married and given birth to two daughters—she was called to work in France. Joan was 'adopted' by a small farming family and lived there for some time while posing as a young teen." I stopped and smiled at Ouriel. "We have great genes in my family and tend to look uncannily teen-like even to thirty."

Ouriel sent me a look of exasperation for my ridiculous boast. "Remain focused, Rose. It is widely known that Guardians have an almost unlimited life span when—"

"When we can actually stay alive that long."

He flushed. "Yes. Please—er—continue with Joan's life after her capture. She was found to be an innocent physically, even though she had been married and given birth, and was still later burned as a witch. Why?"

"That's easy. A small contingent of Warriors and Guardians was dispatched and infiltrated her guards early on. They did all they could to quietly secure her release. They couldn't risk the discovery of our kind, however, and history was allowed to take its course." A sick feeling twisted in my gut.

"What of your grandfather—her husband—and their children?"

"Well, some say he was killed trying to get to her in time. Others say that he went slowly insane and died of a broken heart. But—well…my grandmother always used to say that was a bunch of nonsense."

"Really? Why?"

"Well," I paused for a sip of water, "she said that he clung to both his life and his sanity for his girls. She said he would never have disrespected Joan's life and sacrifice by leaving them alone." I stopped short when my conspicuous lack of knowledge on the subject registered. *Shouldn't we know something? Anything?* "Hmm…that's funny."

"What is funny?"

"Well, I just realized I've never heard much about him or the girls. That's strange, isn't it? Considering there are tons of Warriors still around that knew her? Even Ishmael should at least know what really happened, right? He was the lead Warrior at the time, wasn't he? He must've been in the middle of all of it. You said even you remember that time, and you're thousands of years younger."

"That is true. Have you never asked him about it?"

"No. I never thought to. That *is* really strange." I tried to remember more—any bits or pieces that I might have heard at one time or another. It was weird that, in a family as well documented as mine, I wouldn't know all the facts. Why was there any question at all? I felt Ouriel's gaze weighing on me as he waited for me to work out my thoughts. Unfortunately, like a kid with a math problem way over her head, I couldn't make sense of the whole thing.

"Rose?" Ouriel sounded unwilling to break into my chain of thought.

"Sorry. I'm just trying to understand this stuff. You see, I never really wanted to ask questions when I was younger. I just loved to hear the stories."

"Why did you not ask?"

"I don't know." I paused, searching for a way around my reticence for the subject. It was like an infinite, slippery roadblock with no way through or over it. "The whole thing is like a blank wall to me. There's nothing there."

"Why, do you think?"

"I don't know, Ouriel!" I was beginning to feel suffocated—crushed up against that wall I couldn't see around.

"Think. You *must* know why it bothers you so."

"I told you! I don't know!"

And then the truth crashed over me—it wasn't something I wanted to know. "I guess—I—I don't really want to know." I also didn't want to admit it.

"Why not?"

Resigned to exploring feelings better left buried and rotting, I sighed. "Fine. I loved hearing the stories, but I never asked too many questions or bothered with the particulars because the stories would have become too real. In their generic form, they remained beautiful—even romantic—stories of great personal sacrifice in the name of God. But if I knew too many of the intimate details, if the people in the history became real to me...well...then they became grotesque and horrific tales of the waste of great individuals. And, after my parents died—let's just say it all became too much. My family has paid a huge price in this war for *so* many generations. If I think about it too much, I—I'm afraid I'll lose faith and begin to turn against God," I whispered the last bit, heavy with shame.

The revelations in my confession surprised me. I found I wasn't really ready, even now, to deal with what had just been flushed out of the darkest corners of my mind. It was too shocking, too much against what I had been raised to believe.

Ouriel's silence reverberated in the wake of my quaking admission. I must have seemed weak to him, and I felt seriously mortified. I tried to see myself through his eyes and was greeted with a pathetic picture of a selfish, terribly immature idiot.

"Ouriel, I—" I fumbled. "I'm sorry. That must sound like I'm the weakest, most selfish person ever. I mean—I couldn't *really* lose faith. I know, obviously and without a doubt, that God exists and that I love Him. It's just…oh, I don't know!" I finally gave in and shut myself up because I was totally lost—again. I couldn't bear to see the disapproval that must have shone in his face, so I dropped my head and studied my demon-torn hands instead.

"It is a struggle." Ouriel broke into the quiet with a grim voice. "That is the truth of actual faith. It is never easy. Never completely unshakeable."

Humiliation dragged me down to an even deeper slouch in my seat. *Ouriel is actually trying to comfort me! Ugh.*

"Stop. You don't have to try to make me feel better."

"No. It is you who should stop, Rose. Raise your head and understand this—*all* people of great faith experience doubt in equal measure during the difficult times in their lives. I find it incredibly brave that you can voice those fears. That alone weakens their hold on you. And it demonstrates your willingness to find *true* faith, not merely the appearance of it or the approval of others because of it."

"I never really doubt His existence, you know, but I find myself wondering why God allows things to be the way they are sometimes." I shuddered. "Every now and then, if I let myself, I can get really angry and bitter."

"Rose—" Ouriel leaned toward me. "—you must keep in mind that true faith is not merely believing that God exists. It actually means trusting in the infallibility of His will—a much more difficult objective to achieve al-

together. You must also remember that all God 'allows'
is for each of His beloved creatures to follow his or her
own free will. And that is the greatest, most dangerous
gift that God could give a sentient being."

During his little speech, Ouriel had begun to glow in
my darkening kitchen. Something seemed to give the air
around us a static-like zing, and I felt sucked into the dark
blue of his eyes. His professed admiration of my "courage"—if you could call it that—had left me feeling a little
lighter. And he was right. It felt liberating to voice my
doubts and attempt to master them. It was the same feeling I got after going to Confession—like I was all floaty
and right with the world—if only for the moment.

"Thank you, Ouriel." I fought back the sudden tears
of release that sprang to my eyes. In gratitude, I brushed
the tips of my fingers across the back of the hand he had
rested on the table. Ouriel froze. I saw a spark of heat
catch hold in him once more and, this time, my blood sizzled in response. I couldn't read the expression on Ouriel's face before he sprang to his feet and Jumped away.

I felt only a little bereft in the hush following his abrupt departure. The warm fuzzy of his lingering presence
still surrounded me, as did the cathartic effects of my
confession, but both had left me drained.

I pulled myself up and limped into the kitchen with
our glasses. I dumped their almost untouched contents
into the sink, despite the fact that my dry mouth craved
the coolness they held, and put them in the dishwasher.

My stomach growled its ravenous anger rather audi-
bly, but I ignored it. My day had been entirely too emo-

tional. Complying with my stomach's demands would only make me throw up, so I lugged my exhausted body off to bed. Sleep eluded me, and I fretted for hours with the knowledge that the next day would probably be worse. *Especially if Ouriel persists in forcing me to explore parts of myself I've actively avoided for as long as I've had the choice.*

જ∕જ∕જ

I woke up the next morning even more worn out. After a long wait, I'd finally drifted off—only to witness a bizarre mutation in my nightmare. My mother morphed between herself and Joan of Arc, and my father had been replaced with Ishmael. Since I had no idea what *that* was supposed to mean, I decided to ignore those new little details.

The rest of the dream hadn't changed, especially the demon. In the end, he slithered off into the night like he always did, with only my stifled screams giving chase. I stumbled toward the kitchen. Thanks to his grotesque and lingering presence in my mind, my stomach felt both full of lead and churned up enough to erupt at any moment.

Aggravated with my body's ability to attain such a high state of idiocy, I decided breakfast was out of the question. I seriously needed to gain control of my nerves—and soon—before I ended up looking all lizardy and puckered, like one of those emaciated supermodel-type girls. I shuddered. Some girls might choose to starve themselves, but the women in my family preferred to hone our muscles and revel in the strength of our curves.

Plus, I really liked to eat.

Either way, I needed to chill out.

Before I could force myself to make something for breakfast, I turned to the refrigerator for a drink. Ouriel popped into the kitchen right behind me, and the half-filled cup in my hand shot toward the ceiling. I screeched a terribly embarrassing girly noise, and water spewed everywhere. The orange and white of my giant plastic Whataburger cup swirled across the kitchen then bounced and splashed around the room, finally coming to rest at Ouriel's feet.

My eyes shifted from the floor and offending cup up to a sopping wet Ouriel. His normally glossy auburn hair hung in dripping strings and his shirt clung to his torso. Trying very hard to ignore the wiry muscle I saw there, I focused on his face.

And, much to my dismay, I burst out laughing.

I couldn't even begin to describe what I saw in his expression, but Ouriel's control seemed very much in danger of allowing emotion to snap across his features. I watched him and waited, attempting to rein in my laughter before I died from the ripping streaks of agony in my chest. Ouriel remained perfectly still—well, except for the rivulets of water still coursing down his face.

Slowly, he reached a hand up to his nose and wiped away a stubborn drop of water that seemed determined to hang there, forever suspended. "Good morning. It seems I may have surprised you."

His understatement forced another crack of laughter out of me and had me reaching to squeeze my broken ribs. It took a few moments before I was able to speak.

"Yeah. You could say I was surprised." I bent carefully to pick up my cup. "I don't think my creamsicle glass will ever recover."

"You must be more careful."

"*I* should be more careful? Maybe you shouldn't sneak-Jump right in behind someone! Ow!" Anger rolled through me, and I grabbed for my ribs again.

"I did not sneak-Jump. And *you* should be more aware of your surroundings. In fact, the tactical term for the concept is 'situational awareness.' Learn it."

"Oh! I'm so sorry I'm not situationally aware enough for you! I guess I should just expect people to creep up on me first thing in the morning when I'm minding my own business trying to get a drink of water?"

"Yes, you should. I am glad you admitted it."

"Ouriel, I wasn't saying it was my fault! I was being sarcastic. It was very obviously *your* fault."

"I am well aware of your fondness for sarcasm, Rose, although it seems that you are not able to appreciate the same quality in me." Ouriel headed for the pantry. "Are you hungry? Do you wish to eat before we leave?"

"What? You were kidding?" My mind spun from Ouriel's lightning changes in direction, but I did notice my spurt of anger had burned off most of the nausea I'd been feeling. "Uh, yeah, actually. I guess I am kind of hungry." I handed him a dishtowel to dry off with and turned to grab bowls for cereal just as Miriam staggered into the kitchen.

"Rose, Ouri, you guys need to be careful today." She rubbed her eyes. "I just had a nightmare. You both looked like you'd had the breath sucked out of you, and Javier turned the corner to his shed and found you lying next to one another on the ground."

I instantly tried to quash down the blood in my body before it rushed into my face. I also snuck a glance at Ouriel that confirmed he had begun to glow the orange of a traffic cone. Could she have Seen how Jumping with Ouriel affected me? And then just *mistaken* that for a nightmare? I didn't want to know the answer to either of those questions.

Thankfully, Miriam was too groggy to notice my sudden onset of embarrassment and waited only long enough for both of us to spit out an "Okay!" before she turned and stumbled back to the room she shared with her husband. Ouriel and I both ate our breakfast in an awkward silence, neither saying a word as we prepared to Jump to school.

We arrived there the same way we had the day before—breathless, just as Miriam had seen, and behind Javier's shed. At least, in reality, we landed upright. I wobbled toward the school entrance, still trying to catch my breath, and left Ouriel to find his own way behind me.

Unfortunately, before I could get my locker closed and head for Mrs. Palmer's room, Ana stopped by to whisper cattily, "I see the new boy isn't slumming it yet today. We'll see how long you keep his interest, shy, sweet, little Rose."

I answered her eloquently—with a look of exasperation. Instead of a lame comeback I'd regret later, I kept my mouth shut. Knowing that my silence meant that she'd won the battle, Ana greeted the newly arrived Ouriel and sashayed toward our shared first period. She took great care in her retreat. Rather than paying her the slightest bit of attention, Ouriel aimed a quizzical brow at me. I could only shrug and shake my head in response. I wasn't about to let him in on my latest disgrace so early in the morning.

Our school day passed much like the one before. At lunch, he ate with me again, and Ana didn't bother to come by our table. She chose instead to watch me with slitted eyes from across the cafeteria for the entire hour. The girl definitely had issues—the kind that required the use of really naughty words to describe them properly.

My suffering ended with the final shriek of the school bell. *Ugh*! I thought, when I remembered that my educational torture would only continue when I got home with Ouriel. Already exhausted and aching, I turned and caught a nod from him at his locker, so I headed for our shed. I walked slowly, taking care with my ribs. He was in danger of passing me up if I couldn't move faster, but I was just too tired to try.

I made it to the corner of the little hut and ducked behind it, only to smother a scream when I saw what waited for me there. Miri may have Seen Ouriel and I breathless behind the shed, but Javi lay there, instead, broken and twisted, his once dark brown skin leached of all its magnificent color.

My mind couldn't make sense of the scene in front of me, and I was grabbed up by two strong arms and Jumped away before I could fight back. Panic nearly set in before the smell of Ouriel and incense enveloped me. The two scents calmed me enough to be able to comprehend that it was my Warrior holding me captive and the hard, painful sensation at my back was the wooden floor of the convent chapel.

I opened eyes I hadn't realized were squeezed tight to a vision of cherubim floating cheerily on the chapel ceiling. My breath came in labored pants, but I couldn't grab for my ribs because Ouriel's body was still crushing me into the floor.

"Rose," he shouted, "Rose, are you all right?"

"Yes." I choked on a sob. "But Javi—what about Javi?"

"I am going to get him right now. Do not move," Ouriel ordered, jostling me as he rose to Jump. Misery shot through my body so intensely that his words hardly registered in my mind.

I tried to sit up, but I hurt so badly that I could only manage to drag myself onto a nearby pew and lay there. I noticed then that tears snaked down my face. The tears weren't for myself—I knew I was entirely safe in God's house—they were for Javier.

What had happened to him? Was he dead? *Stop being childish*, my brain told me.

I knew he was dead.

I just didn't know what—or who—had killed him.

All thought disintegrated when Ouriel Jumped back in with the body of my old friend and a freaked out Shadrach.

"Rose! Are you okay?" Shad grated out as soon as he landed, snatching me up in an awkward hug that nearly caused me to black out in pain.

"Yes," I moaned into his shoulder. "I'm just hurting, but Javi—Javi—" I turned and saw Ouriel lay Javier's corpse down on a pew.

"I know, sweetie. You must be really scared right now. But don't worry. I'm going to take care of him. A contingent of Guardians is already in place to secure the school grounds. No one else will be hurt today."

Ouriel strode away from the pew and plucked me out of my brother-in-law's arms. "It is time I take Rose home."

"Why?" The whiny quality in my own voice disgusted me. "What about Javi? What the hell happened to him?"

"I will answer all of your questions in the safety of your home." Ouriel nodded at Shad and took only a moment to gather me more securely in his arms before blinking us out of the silence of the chapel and into the chaos of my kitchen.

"Ouriel! Oh, thanks be to God! She's okay!" Miriam's cry blended with Genevieve's, "Thank Heaven! I wasn't sure! I'd received word, but, Ouri, I'm so glad you were right there!"

I took a deep breath, not only to check my own wild heartbeat, but also in an attempt to gain some control over my surroundings.

"Miriam. Gen. I am fine. My ribs are just hurting. That's all." I looked up at Ouriel, who showed no sign of releasing me. "If you'd put me down, please, I would appreciate it. Thank you. Now, if you don't mind, I'd like to lie down in the living room while you all answer some questions for me." I was nearing my overload threshold and didn't wait for a reply before turning toward the blessed comfort of the leather couch beckoning from the other room.

Ouriel beat me there and sat just where I liked to lay my head, so I slumped down at the other end of the couch and tried in vain to control the shivering of my body. I knew I was nearing a breakdown because of what I'd witnessed only minutes before, but I felt desperate to keep it together long enough to get more information. I preferred to lose my mind in solitude.

Miriam and Gen followed us into the living room and busied themselves with casting worried glances at one another. I looked from my sisters to Ouriel and wondered which of them was most incapable of providing me comfort at the moment. The Warrior was boring holes into my body with eyes that pored over every inch of me, in search of some non-existent damage, and neither of my sisters seemed able to even look me in the eye.

Sick of waiting for someone else to break the silence and still too rattled to think coherently for myself, I finally asked, "Um—is *anyone* going to explain to me what just happened to Javi?"

Miriam and Gen both hesitated to answer, so Ouriel spoke. "What you just witnessed was the aftermath or the shell of a human being that remains after his or her soul has been devoured by a demon."

"Demon?" I whispered, not sure I truly understood. "What? You mean a demon was at school today? A demon stole Javi's soul?" My voice reached a nearly hypersonic level with the last question. "But it can't be! I thought the school was protected!"

"It was."

"Then how did this happen? How come no one was there to save him?"

"I do not yet know. I devised what I thought was seamless coverage of the grounds. The fact that there was no sighting of this demon is worrisome. Even more so is the location of the attack—an area recently frequented by you."

"So? Who cares about that? I want to know why Javi's dead!"

Greeted once more by my sisters' silence, Ouriel stepped in again. "That is what I am attempting to elucidate for you, Rose. We do not know why—at the moment. We can only guess that he was very likely working in or around his shed and his body was left purposely at our Jump spot. I fear this signifies that you are in even graver danger than we had imagined."

"But you can't know that for sure, Ouri," Gen gasped.

"I can. The only common denominator in the last two demon sightings has been Rose. The simplest conclusion must be that she is the demonic draw."

"No way!" I refused to consider that Ouriel might be right. "There is no way this is about me. There must be someone else. Another kid at school, maybe. Or a Guardian or Warrior in the contingent."

After a pensive pause, Ouriel countered, "I do not believe so."

"Ouriel, what Rose is saying may make some sense." Miriam crossed over to stand by me. "It's not very likely that demons would be concerned with a Sightless Guardian. Is it possible that one of ours may have been turned?"

"Again, I do not believe that is the case, and neither should you. You cannot allow your fear for Rose to cloud your judgment. Think, Miriam, if one of us had been turned, while his or her appearance would remain unchanged in the eyes of the Sightless at Father Yermo, we would have already begun to witness the transformation."

"Not if it occurred within the last hour," Gen put in.

"You're right, Gen," Miriam interjected. "We need an accountability report of all Guardians and Warriors assigned to the vicinity of south El Paso immediately. I'll Jump down to the school myself. I want to hear personally what Shad has discovered so far."

Gen moved to go with her. "Will you need any help?"

"I'm not sure. It's bound to be mayhem down there, though, between student pick up and trying to stay as inconspicuous as possible to the Sightless, so I really might—"

"Genevieve—" Ouriel jumped in. "—if you two are insistent upon remaining on this futile track, you should go with Miriam. You will be forced to see the reality of my conclusions that much quicker. I will remain here with Rose."

"Are you sure?" Gen looked hesitant. "Rose, baby, do you need me to stay? I can if you want."

"No, Gen. I'll be all right. You go. I just kind of want to be left to myself tonight anyway." I couldn't believe I sounded so composed. I was battling to keep my signs of hysteria to a minimum in front of my infinitely more resilient older sisters, but my mind was in chaos. My thoughts churned and tripped over themselves in their attempts to be heard.

"Are you sure?"

"I'm sure, Genevieve. Go. Both of you. Make sure this doesn't happen to anyone else. And find out why it *did* happen to Javi. I hope to God it truly had nothing to do with me."

"Okay, dear," Miriam whispered. "If that's what you want."

"It is."

Miriam leaned over to hug me. "Well, then, I love you."

"Bye, baby sister," Gen said, blowing me a kiss over the top of Miriam.

Normally, I protested when subjected to Miriam's physical affections, but tonight I found a sweet comfort in her arms. "I love you too, Miri. Bye, Gen. And thank you both."

CHAPTER 5

"Are you all right?" Ouriel asked after my sisters Jumped away.

"I'm fine," I bit off, more tersely than I should have. "Sorry. I'm still a little freaked. And I'm hurting too."

"You must lie down," Ouriel commanded.

"Um—I should—but you've commandeered the only full couch in the room, and I don't feel like being exiled to my bedroom this early in the day."

"You may lie down here." Ouriel patted the open area on the couch near him. "Once you have rested a moment, we can discuss today's events in greater detail."

"I don't want to rest, Ouriel. I just want to know what happened. Javi was a good person!" I exploded. "He was just a little old man, eeking out a living as a caretaker."

"Please, Rose, calm yourself. I know that his loss pains you greatly, but you must rest. You are still healing from your own demonic encounter."

The reminder of my own close call with a demon drained the fight right out of me. I wasn't sure if it was the concern evident in Ouriel's voice, the fact that he had actually asked me to be near him, or sheer exhaustion on my part, but the need to lie down overwhelmed me. I sank down onto the cushions of the sofa.

I laid my head on the arm opposite Ouriel and curled my legs up to my chest as closely as possible, forming a tight little ball with my body. It was imperative that not one molecule of my being come into contact with the Warrior so close to me. I didn't think I could handle feeling even one more sensation of any kind or I would rupture from emotional overload.

Unfortunately, the last of my self-control eroded anyway, and I could no longer keep leashed the sobs that threatened to rip my body in half. Between ragged breaths, I managed to moan out a pathetic "Why?" to Ouriel.

In answer, he placed his hand on my knee and said simply, "I cannot pretend to know the will of the Father, Rose."

I couldn't respond before the intense warmth of his touch flooded through me, and I floated fitfully off to sleep.

ເຈເຈເຈ

True to my curse, a nightmare trapped me yet again. I fell and fell without respite. No matter how I flailed and struggled, I couldn't seem to break free of the invisible iron cage of despair that would inevitably crush me into dust. Just as I felt I was going to implode, my eyes snapped open to find Ouriel staring at me intently, his face squarely in mine with his body pinning my own to the couch. I stilled and fought to orient myself.

"Are you fully awakened, Rose?" he panted.

"Yes. I think so. What the heck just happened?" I was suffocating from the combination of his weight and the sting in my ribcage. "Um—do you think you can get off me now? I can't breathe."

Half the pain tearing through my chest evaporated instantly. Ouriel was now upright and scanning my every movement. For once, he didn't seem at all unsettled by our previous bodily proximity. His face was filled only with concern and what seemed to be a hint of confusion.

"I apologize for having restrained you, but you seemed intent on doing me physical damage."

And, of course, it was me who ended up mortified.

"I did *what*?"

"You attacked me. And I must say, with only a bit more training, you might very well have succeeded in truly harming me."

"Yeah, right. Only in my dreams am I capable of hurting you." The idea was ludicrous. "How long was I asleep?"

"Approximately four hours."

"No way!" I screeched, searching for the nearest clock. I found it on the cable box above our television and was shocked to see that it read a few minutes after eight. "Ohmygosh. I didn't mean to sleep that long. Why didn't you wake me up? I've got homework to do!" I started to get up only to have Ouriel push me back down onto the couch.

"Rose, for someone in your condition, rest is always the top priority. You can complete your homework in a moment. I will fetch your backpack from the kitchen, along with some food for you."

"Uh...okay. Thanks." Wow. That was another truly eloquent turn of phrase for me to pass on to posterity. Well, I *had* had a bad day, though not nearly as bad as Javi's. I winced at the last memory I'd ever have of him as a lifeless, broken shell of a human behind that shed. *Maybe you should go a little easier on yourself*, a voice from somewhere in the back of my mind shouted. Life had played a bit rough with me lately.

I had no more time to debate with myself when Ouriel walked into the room with my pack over his shoulder, a peanut butter and jelly sandwich and chips on a plate, and a glass of milk in his hand. My stomach roared an ecstatic welcome to the simple feast he'd brought in.

Without speaking, I devoured everything on the plate and in the glass and felt sated for the first time in what seemed like forever.

Ouriel didn't speak until I finished eating. "We will skip Guardian training tonight in deference to your need to rest and to complete your Sightless assignments. However, I to wish address what happened earlier with Javier."

I responded by grabbing my dishes and ducking into the kitchen. I rinsed my plate and glass and put them in the dishwasher.

Ouriel followed me, obviously sensing that I was stalling for time. "Are you not ready to discuss this?"

Despite my earlier declarations to the contrary, I found myself suddenly unwilling to know the details of what had befallen one of the few people I considered my friend.

"You know what, Ouriel? I don't really need to know. Let's just skip it for now and pick it up tomorrow when I feel better. Tell me instead if you've heard anything from Miriam and Genevieve."

"Rose—" Ouriel skewered me with a glare, "—do not allow yourself this cowardice. You must face what happened today. Do not hide from it now that you have had an opportunity to recover your wits."

"Cowardice?" I tried to work myself into a self-righteous rage for which I really didn't have the energy. I knew he was right. My life was always easier when I could trick myself into thinking things weren't as bad as they seemed. I also realized, in a small epiphany, that I was quite accomplished at it. I'd never recognized the tendency before, but it was glaring to me now that Ouriel had called me out on it. "Ha! Who am I trying to kid? You're right. I am a coward. Just tell me what you have to so I can deal with it already."

"I did not call you a coward. I simply stated that you could not allow yourself the weakness you have in the past. You must learn to deal intellectually with evil because, no matter how you try to avoid it, it will find you. Wherever you may choose to hide."

"I already said you were right, Ouriel, so tell me already!" If I was going to have to face evil, I wanted to do it quickly and have the whole thing over with.

"Very well, then. As I already told you, the shell of a human being you saw today behind the shed was all that remained of the caretaker, Javier. No one, more specifically, no non-demon, knows just what happens to a soul once it is consumed."

"What do you mean, no one knows?" I interrupted. "How can Warriors not know? Isn't there something in one of those Sacred Books you guys keep hidden around and never let anyone read?"

"No, there is no writing that can answer the question. It is a great mystery which the Father has not yet chosen to reveal to any of His beings." Ouriel bowed his head at those words and then continued, "We have theories, educated guesses, but that is all."

"So what are the theories?"

"Well, we know a few things to be fact. For example, the soul of the human attacked ceases to exist on any plane known to celestial beings. It does not pass on to any area of the celestial realm, nor does it exist among the demon horde. It seems that the soul is completely destroyed, and we are left to conclude that nothingness is its destiny."

"But that's so sad." Talk about an understatement. "Can God really allow that?"

"As I said, none of us knows what truly happens to the soul. We only know that we must trust the Creator, even when we do not understand His plan or purpose. We must know, we must *believe*, that He can work even these greatest of evils to His good."

"I don't like it, Ouriel. The whole idea makes me sick."

Rather than answer me, he slowly, deliberately, pulled me up from where I had leaned to rest on the kitchen counter and gathered me into a hug. I'm not sure which one of us was more shocked by such a display of affection from him. Rather than immediately Jumping away in embarrassment, Ouriel whispered in my ear, "Now you know how truly amazing are those who remain faithful even in their discomfort. You, too, will be one of those few, Rose. God will use you to bring about a portion of His will here on earth."

I shivered and closed my eyes as Ouriel trailed his fingers down a single strand of my ponytail. By the time I shifted to catch a glimpse of his face, the Warrior was gone.

ﻭﻭﻭ

I awoke the next morning filled with guilt because I knew I shouldn't have fallen asleep so easily or slept so well the night before. I couldn't help it, though. Even engulfed in shame, my body still tingled with the memory of my last encounter with Ouriel. I chastised myself for reveling in last night's small gesture from him—so much so that I'd been able to disregard, selfishly, the evil that had stolen a man's life only hours before.

Javier deserved better. Especially from me. Frustrated, I swiped at the tears threatening to slide down my cheeks and resolved to remain more focused. It was not the time to indulge in idiotic teenage fantasies. I forced myself to prepare for school and even managed to choke down a bowl of cereal before Ouriel strode into the kitchen.

"Good morning. Did you sleep well?"

"As a matter of fact, I did. Thank you. How was your night?" I didn't ask if he had slept well, knowing that, although they did sleep, Warriors required little rest to recuperate.

"Active. We are still investigating Javier's death. We have found no leads as of yet, which only adds to the mystery. Something should have presented itself at this point." Ouriel's irritation rang through the room.

"You guys haven't found anything? At all?"

"I am afraid not. However, you and I must attend classes today and appear to believe nothing is out of sorts."

"I figured. Does the school know anything? About Javi being dead?"

"No. And none of our kind will enlighten them. They will have to draw conclusions of their own or contact the Sightless Police Department."

"That sucks. Javi dedicated his life to caring for that school. And now he won't even get the sendoff he deserves because none of the Sightless will know the truth. It isn't fair."

"No, Rose, it is not. However, *you* know what happened, and you are able to mourn and commemorate him in your own way."

"You're right." A tiny bit of my anger burned away. Maybe no one else would celebrate Javi's life, but I could. I could do *something* to remember him. I didn't know what yet, but I would figure it out eventually.

"Are you ready to leave?"

"Yes," I breathed, instantly sidetracked by the memory of the last time Ouriel had touched me. *Nope*! I refused to morph into some insipid teenage girl and devote my attention to trivial things. I stepped into Ouriel's arms and concentrated on finding a way to honor Javi's memory.

As we arrived at our new landing spot, the ferocious stink of the dumpster in the school parking lot accosted my nostrils. I shied away from touching the nasty thing as I walked out of the narrow space between it and the building that bordered the lot. Nothing else—other than a whiff of the horrendous smell I could swear clung to me—interrupted the tedium of my morning.

My morning classes blurred together in a haze of depression. Each time I caught Ouriel's eyes watching me, my stomach fluttered and guilt set in. His whispered words the night before had changed something inside me, and I wasn't ready to explore what it might be. The death and devastation of the last few days had ruptured the fabric of my life, and my burgeoning infatuation had no place in it.

When it was time for lunch, Ouriel joined me in the walk across the burning asphalt basketball courts and playgrounds on our way to the cafeteria we shared with the elementary and middle schools. It felt good to have someone to talk to for once—not to mention the fact that this someone could actually understand the realities of how I lived. With him, I'd never have to lie or pretend when it came to the insanity that pervaded every aspect of my life.

After Ouriel and I picked up our lunches, we sat down to eat, and I noticed Ana making a beeline for us. *Crap.* I really couldn't stand that girl. She was a total pain. It took all of my self-control not to wince when she arrived at our table, and I couldn't help bracing mentally for impact.

"Your name is Ouriel, right?" Ana asked him, mispronouncing his name horribly. Ouriel nodded. "Well, Ouriel, if you want, you can come sit over there with me and my friends." She pointed to a table on the opposite side of the cafeteria. "I know you've only been here a few days, but we're the best group to hang with at lunch. You really wouldn't want to sit anywhere else."

She cast a sly look in my direction before blasting Ouriel with her most beguiling smile. Despite her efforts, I still sensed malice oozing from her every sweat gland.

There was nothing I could do but watch and wait for Ouriel's response. I had a sick feeling in my stomach. I knew that, on the inside, Ana was an ugly human being. Outwardly, however, she was downright gorgeous.

Physically, I'd never be on a level with Ana and her friends, so I reminded myself that, when it came to brains, they would never be able to compete with me. The wait for Ouriel's answer was beginning to frazzle me. I didn't think he'd leave me to sit with the other kids, but I couldn't control the overwhelming doubts that ate at me as Ana and I pretended to wait patiently for him to speak.

After a moment of tense silence, Ouriel's face contorted with distaste. "Just because a person believes she is superior in company does not make it so. As it is, if I must choose between a vapid girl such as yourself and one as beautiful and intelligent as I have found Rose to be, it is no choice at all." He turned his back on Ana and dug into his *enchiladas* as if the conversation had never occurred.

I stared at Ana as she tried to make sense of the words Ouriel had just spoken. I stifled a laugh because she couldn't seem to decide if she had been insulted or not, and her confusion continued for a full thirty seconds. In the end, she threw me a disgusted look, turned on her heel, and stalked back to her table. She must have finally figured out that vapid wasn't a synonym for good looking.

ↃↄↃↄ

The rest of the afternoon passed uneventfully, and I trudged back to my locker when the final bell rang. Ever since the confrontation at lunch, my stomach did back

handsprings whenever I looked at Ouriel. I couldn't believe he'd called me beautiful, even offhandedly.

I closed my locker and slung my backpack over one
shoulder, and Ouriel caught my eye from across the hall.
I knew he wanted me to walk ahead of him to the parking
lot dumpster, but I was having trouble keeping my attention on even that simple task. My palms were sweating in
anticipation of the trip back to my house, and my feelings
for Ouriel were spiraling way out of control. I found all
of it a bit irritating. *One or two casual compliments and
I'm a puddle at his feet. Disgusting.* I just hoped I could
play it cool a little longer—or at least until Ish got back. I
turned my mind to Javier in order to keep myself ground-
ed.

We got to our spot, and Ouriel wouldn't meet my
gaze when we took hold of one another in preparation for
the Jump. His silence told me that he had withdrawn even
more completely into himself than I'd seen him do before, and I didn't know why. I *had* thought for a moment
that we were becoming friends, especially after the night
before. Secretly, I had also begun to hope—against
hope—that we might become even more. But his cold
indifference throughout the afternoon told me he had re-
verted to being irritated with, or at least annoyed by, me.
So much for being beautiful only two hours ago. I
laughed at myself. I was really good at self-delusion.

Reeling from the realization that his earlier defense
of me had probably been for appearances only, I muttered
to Ouriel, "I just wanted to—you know—say thank you.
For what you said to Ana at lunch today. I know you

were just being nice, but it—well…anyway—I appreciate it."

"I spoke nothing more or less than the truth, Rose. I was not just 'being nice.' You have no need to thank me," he snapped. "Now, come. Let us return you to your home."

Without thinking, I burrowed my face into his chest so he couldn't see the feelings in my eyes. Emotion for this Warrior, whom I couldn't seem to understand, overwhelmed me. I only knew that he made me feel safer and more comfortable with myself than I ever had before, but it seemed I was just another burden to him.

The sensation from Jumping always left me gasping for air with Ish. With Ouriel, I was breathless for an entirely different reason. Without opening my eyes, I knew by smell alone when we arrived at my house. Before letting go of him, I looked up at Ouriel. I couldn't stop the single tear that fell from my eye to flow down my cheek.

The last few days had been too much. My ribs still hurt when I moved too quickly. I felt like my whole chest would rip apart with the force of all the tears I had yet to shed, for Javi, for myself, and for Ishmael. *God help me*! I missed Ish.

Ouriel wiped the tear from my face with his thumb. He had a look of tenderness in his eyes I had never seen there before, even last night in my kitchen. "Rose," he whispered, "you will be the death of me yet."

I thought for a crazy, giddy, stupid second that he was going to kiss me.

I was wrong.

Ouriel wrenched himself out of my arms. "If you must cry, please do so elsewhere. And do be quick about it. We need to continue your lessons. You have ten minutes before I will expect you on the back porch."

He turned his back on me, just as he had Ana, and stomped to the back of our house. I stood, frozen, where he had left me.

The slam of the back door shattered my mental paralysis. I hurried down the hallway and flung my bedroom door closed loudly enough—I hoped—for him to hear it outside.

The tears came in earnest then, and I threw myself onto the bed. I didn't understand what that scene in the front hall had been about. For that matter, I didn't understand Ouriel at all. One moment, he was sweet and kind—the next, he was rude and unbearable.

I missed Ishmael. I missed the peaceful life that had been mine not so long ago. *I don't even know how Ish is doing*! Whenever I asked, Miriam would tell me not to worry, that Warriors healed quickly—as if she were talking to a child.

I decided that I'd had enough. I might or might not be in danger from demons, but that was no reason for me to lose total control of my own life.

I stormed out of my bedroom and headed for the back porch. Ouriel stood at the edge of the patio, staring ahead blankly. When I let the screen door bang behind me, his head snapped around in my direction.

"Good. You are ready then."

"Yes, I'm ready," I shouted. "I'm ready to let you and everybody else around here know that I'm sick of the way you all act around me. Miriam treats me like a five-year-old. Gen treats me like a spoiled brat who doesn't care about anything but herself. And you—I don't even know what to say to you! You're nice and sweet one minute, calling me beautiful and intelligent, and the next minute, you act like I have some kind of plague that might infect you!"

Ouriel stared at me like he'd never seen me before. His mouth might even have dropped open for half a second. In the next moment, he stood directly in front of me, furious. He pulled me close to him and held me up so our gazes were level with one another. I could see the anger boiling in him.

His voice was deadly when he gritted out, "You are neither spoiled, nor are you a brat. And I can only wish you were a child because you *are* like a disease to me. You alternately infuriate and entrance me. I cannot wait until Ishmael has recovered so I can be rid of you."

"Fine! You can be rid of me right now." I tore myself out of his grasp and headed for the front door. I pushed past Gen on my way and never stopped to see if Ouriel followed me.

"Rose—Rose!" She called after me as I ran down the hallway. "What is going on? I heard you and Ouriel yelling. Is everything okay?"

I didn't hesitate on my way out the door and slammed it closed behind me. I ran out the gate, across the street, and quickly turned the corner. None of them could Jump after me if they didn't know where I was. I checked behind me and saw no one. I slowed to a walk to keep my ribs from killing me, continued on a bit farther, and crossed another street. At the next intersection, I turned again and stopped for a moment. I couldn't go on because I couldn't see. My vision had blurred with more tears. I swatted at the moisture in my eyes. *Why can't I freaking stop crying?*

Stupid Ouriel. Stupid Gen. Stupid demons. I hated my whole stupid life. Why couldn't I have been born into a normal family?

I headed for a huge, deserted lot across the street, one like so many others that dotted the older neighborhoods like mine in El Paso, and sat on a rock behind a sand dune. I gave in to the full force of my self-pity and sobbed. I don't know how long I sat like that before I heard footsteps squelching up beside me in the dirt. I looked up, humiliated, expecting to see one of my sisters or Ouriel.

Instead, I saw a demon.

He was disguised as a homeless man, but I could feel the evil surging from him. I sat paralyzed, watching him come closer to me. Then I caught his scent. The smell of decaying flesh nearly overcame me.

I was entirely alone and defenseless.

I jumped up and backed away from him, stumbling. Panic beckoned me to collapse in fear. An evil grin crept across his face, revealing his blackened gums.

"Your soul smells awfully good, little one," he hissed at me. "I think I might fancy a taste of it."

"Stay away from me," I said with as much bravado as I could muster.

"Why should I? The scent of your soul is calling to me. It wouldn't hurt for me to have just a little taste—" He broke off and lunged for me.

I ducked and sprinted back the way I had come. I just had to make it home. It was my only chance at escape. Even after my ribs felt like they had cracked again, I kept running. I dodged, turning left and right, so the demon couldn't Jump in front of me and block my escape. He would have no choice but to run after me. His ragged breathing grew louder as he gained on me, aided by my limping stride.

Agony ripped through my back as the demon tackled me from behind. I knew that my ribs had broken again, and I was pretty sure my arm did too when I crashed to the ground. The demon flipped me over, so I faced him. He sat, straddling me, and pressed my arms into the blistering hot sand.

I couldn't breathe. My arm and ribs screamed in protest, but they soon faded into the background. Mesmerized by the demon's eyes as he bent his head toward mine, I saw his face twist and reshape itself to reflect my own. I felt the demon's lips touch my temple and shivered in fear. As he tried to tear my soul from me, my last thoughts were of Ouriel.

"You idiot!" I heard a female's muffled scream. "You can't eat her soul! She's of Guardian blood. She's the one we're after!"

I heard the zing of a blade and the weight of the demon was lifted off my chest. His body flew about twenty feet to my right, but his head remained, dripping and severed, just to the side of me. I couldn't command myself to look away and watched with disgust as his face settled back into its natural contours.

Had the demoness chopped his head off? *Holy crap!*

I needed to get up and run, but my body refused to cooperate. I was in excruciating pain and couldn't seem to move my legs. I finally managed to look to my left and saw the female leader from the other night locked in battle with Ouriel. Relief poured through me.

He must have beheaded the male. I sent up a silent prayer of thanksgiving. I didn't know how he had found me, and I didn't care. My eyes blurred while I watched the sunlight glance off his sword as it sliced back and forth, nearly catching the female with every strike. Each time, however, she dodged the blade just before the blow landed. Meanwhile, she gouged at him with her claws.

Finally, Ouriel spun and slashed, hitting her at the shoulder and nearly amputating her arm. It remained, only to dangle limply at her side. She turned and ran, realizing that she was hopelessly outmatched. All she needed was a few feet of space to Jump, so she spread her wings and took flight. When the demoness was about ten feet in the air, her body swirled into nothingness.

Ouriel searched our immediate surroundings before he bent to the male demon's body. It burst into blue flame with a slight touch of his palm. He proceeded to move the demon's head a short distance away from me and did the same to it. When the fires had burned out, which they did surprisingly fast, Ouriel finally turned to look at me.

His eyes burned with same bluish white flames that had just cremated the demon.

The ferocity in him terrified me. I had sensed great power within Ouriel at times, but seeing it in action was downright menacing. He loped back to me. Without saying a word, he picked me up with an aching gentleness that belied the blaze in his eyes. Agony tore through me, and everything faded to black.

CHAPTER 6

The shouts of my sisters yanked me back to consciousness. I didn't know for sure, but I guessed that Ouriel had Jumped us back to my house. I couldn't seem to get my eyes all the way open. My body burned all over—especially my abdomen, where the demon had sat on top of me.

"Is she all right?" Gen gasped.

"Oh, my God!" Miriam sounded like she was going to faint. "What happened, Ouriel?"

"Rose is severely injured. She was under attack. There were two demons—a fairly new one and the female leader from Friday night."

"I'll have Shad contact a Healer right now." I felt Gen rush for the door.

"No!" Ouriel shouted. I heard the scuffles of my sisters backing away from him in shock. "I'm sorry," he continued, more subdued. "What I mean to say is that I will care for her injuries. Her condition is entirely my fault."

"What are you going to do? You're not going to—"

"Yes, I am." Ouriel cut Miriam off.

"But, Ouri," Gen interjected, "you can't. You may lose yourself in the process. Let us call a Healer—"

"I have made up my mind. Her injuries are too extensive. Her back is broken, and I can See internal bleeding. She will not survive if I do not do this," Ouriel choked out. I wanted to protest along with my sisters, but I didn't know what they were talking about and my body wouldn't respond to any of my commands. "I need you both to leave the room. Please."

I felt the shifting of air as someone walked out. I realized it must have been Gen when I heard Miriam say, "I'm sorry, Ouriel, but I am not leaving either one of you. I have seen this done before, and I will not distract you. I want to be here, in case of—well—just in case."

"All right, you can stay, but do not disturb me in any way. It may cost both Rose and me our lives." Ouriel lowered me onto the couch in our living room. "By the way, where is Shadrach?"

"He is already gone to inform your father. We weren't sure if you were going to need back up, or if Rose would even be found." From the corner of my eye, I saw Miriam swipe her hair out of her eyes and dig her fingertips into her scalp. "I can't believe she just ran off like that."

"As I stated earlier, the fault was mine, and I do not wish to discuss the matter further. When my father arrives, if something has gone wrong, let him know that Rose was my only concern. I would not want to live in a world where she did not." Ouriel's voice broke with that final statement.

"Ouri," Miriam breathed in a cracked whisper.

Ouriel ignored Miriam's sympathy. "It is time."

"Okay," I heard her say.

Whether she moved or not, I will never know because I felt a marvelous warmth shoot through me. Ouriel had pressed his hands onto my stomach, and slivers of what felt like electricity bolted out from where he touched me. My ribs no longer hurt, and the pressure in my abdomen ceased.

"I am sorry, Rose," a voice echoed in my head. It was Ouriel's. "I did not mean to hurt you."

The words exploded within me, and I was suddenly with the Warrior himself. His presence surrounded me. He was in me, around me, and through me. I felt him in every cell of my being. I wondered what he was doing to me and simultaneously hoped it would never stop. For once, all of the suffering, both physical and emotional, had left my body.

"Thank you," I murmured and, ever so slowly, I felt Ouriel drift away from me and his hands slip off my abdomen. I awoke with a jolt, my eyes popping open in desperate search of his. Instead, I locked onto Miriam's gaze, where I saw confirmation that something had gone terribly wrong.

It seemed like an eternity before I found Ouriel. He lay motionless on the floor, just below me. I slid down to his side, and Miriam rushed over to join me. We knelt over him. Even in the gloom of the unlit room, I was able to make out the mangled condition of Ouriel's body. The sun must have set while I lay unconscious, and it struck me that Ouriel's golden skin should have dispelled the shadows surrounding us.

"Miriam, what do we do?"

"I don't know—"

"What do you *mean* you don't know?"

"Rose, I've seen Warriors lay their hands on others before, so I do know that he has taken on all your injuries. But that's all I know. Remember, Warriors mend differently than we do, *especially* their Healers." Miriam sighed. "For now, all we can do is wait."

"*Wait*? Are we just supposed to sit here and watch him die?"

"We don't know that he's going to die. Wait and watch. The last thing he told me was not to distract him." Miriam's tone brooked no further argument.

I felt impotent, kneeling there, watching Ouriel suffer the pain that should rightfully have been mine. I was the moron who had run out alone. *Gah*! I was so stupid. For days, people had been telling me I was in danger. Ouriel himself had instructed me not to leave the house without him. Of course, in my idiocy, I had believed myself safe. Seriously though, what would anyone want with me—least of all demons? In hindsight, I could have slapped myself. I didn't know *why* they wanted me, but there was no doubt that it was *me* they wanted. I swore to myself then that I would never be caught off guard again.

Ouriel has to be okay! I needed him—and not just for protection. In the last week or so, he had somehow become necessary to my existence. I'd grown accustomed to seeing him nearby every time I looked for him. I stared down at Ouriel's beautiful, angelic face and kissed his cheek. He had risked his life for me, and I knew he felt ridiculously responsible for what had happened to me tonight.

I would be dead if it weren't for this Warrior, lying on my living room floor, fighting for his life. A tear slid down my cheek, tumbled over my jaw, and landed on his chest. I knew then, irrevocably, that any hopes of not making a fool of myself over him were lost.

I was totally in love with him.

No. I shook my head. *No way*!

I'd known him for too short a time! The rational part of my brain rebelled, screaming that it was too soon for me to be truly in love with Ouriel. People didn't fall in love that fast. Not smart people, anyway. The idea that I already felt so much for him was ridiculous, ludicrous even.

Yet, there it was.

I couldn't shake the sentiment, no matter how hard I tried to beat some sense into myself. The emotion was so much bigger than I was. There was no denying it.

I didn't know what else to do, so I lay down next to Ouriel and wrapped my arms around him as best I could. The physical contact felt right, so I rested my head on his chest, listening for his heartbeat.

"I don't think you should do that—"

"Miriam, for once in your life, shut up and trust me!"

"It's just that—" Miriam whispered. "Well, I've known Ouri for a long time, and he doesn't like to be touched. I don't want anything to hurt his chances of beating this."

"Look, he's the one that chose to lay hands on me. Now I'm going to do the same for him. Unfortunately, I can't do much more than keep him warm," I muttered bitterly, snuggling even closer to him. His breath escaped in ragged bursts.

Miriam paced the floor and left me alone. I tried to concentrate on Ouriel and forget everything else. I closed my eyes and focused on the way he had made me feel in the short time since he had come into my life. I thought about the unexpected kindnesses he had shown me, and the way his arms felt holding me during a Jump. I also thought of the way he had defended me in the cafeteria this afternoon. It seemed years ago now, but my breath still caught at the memory of his calling me beautiful and smart. My mind heatedly recalled how his hands had felt, just a few minutes ago, spreading life back into my body.

The sound of a commotion in the front hallway broke my concentration, and it fractured completely when the noise broke into the room along with a formidable older Warrior. Gen and Shad trailed behind him, both looking helpless. The Warrior's gaze met Miriam's first, as she stood frozen near the window. Then the full intensity of it smashed into me. The stricken look in his eyes morphed quickly into shock when he saw me cradling Ouriel. I trembled with the realization that this newly arrived Warrior was merely an older version of the one in my arms.

"How is he?" the Warrior demanded.

"We don't know." To her credit, Miriam's voice didn't quaver. "I know Rose's injuries were severe. Ouriel said that she had massive internal bleeding and a broken back. We wanted to summon a Healer, but he wouldn't let us. He insisted that she wouldn't last until one got here."

"I understand." He dismissed Miriam like a wayward servant. "Thank you. I do not hold you responsible. Ouriel knew the risk he was assuming. He also knew that it was entirely unnecessary. The girl would have survived long enough for a Healer to arrive. Now excuse me. All of you. I will take matters from here."

I didn't budge from Ouriel's side.

"Rose, come with me, honey." Miriam moved to pull me up and away from Ouriel. "This is Briathos, Ouriel's father. He will care for him now."

"I'm not going anywhere."

"If you please, young lady." Briathos's superior tone grated on my ears. It sounded so similar to his son's I nearly let out a laughing sob. "I assure you I am much more qualified to care for my son than you. He needs quiet to heal right now. You must leave."

"I. Am. Not. Leaving."

"Young lady, I have no wish to argue with you, but I really must insist—"

"Ouriel needs me!" I broke in. "I am going *nowhere*. He risked his life twice for me tonight, and I know the only thing that can help him now is for me to be close to him. Don't ask me how I know it—I just do!" My eyes flew from one of my sisters to the other, searching out any kind of support I might find. I wrestled back a panic of tears before anyone could use them against me.

"Very well," Briathos relented. "I will allow you to remain with him, but I *would* like to make him more comfortable." I got up as Briathos came forward and lifted Ouriel into his arms.

"Wait. Don't put him on the couch," Gen called out. "Please. Use my room. I have a big enough bed for him."

Briathos nodded, and we followed her down the long hallway, past my room, to hers.

The sage green room was obsessively neat, unlike mine. The sleigh bed was king sized and built in a dark cherry wood. The dresser and nightstands matched perfectly. Briathos laid Ouriel on the bed and turned to me. I took the hint and scrambled across the bed to curl around Ouriel once more.

Miriam, Shad, and Gen left the room. I left it to Briathos to break the deafening silence first.

"Your name is Rose, correct?"

"Yes, sir."

Briathos's eyes raked over me. "Do you know how rare it is for a Warrior to lay his hands on a human, Guardian or not?"

"No, sir. I have no formal Guardian training."

"Well, my dear, it is very extraordinary indeed and is rarely done, even in the direst of circumstances. It seems to me that even as extensive as your injuries were, you could have survived until a Guardian Healer was able to Jump in to attend you."

I didn't reply. I had no idea what point the Warrior was trying to make.

"Yes, on the whole, I believe that it was entirely unnecessary for Ouriel to put himself in this position." Briathos paused to walk across the room to stare out the window. "Ouriel, however, does not act rashly. Nor has he touched others or allowed anyone to touch him since his mother's death nearly 500 years ago. Why, do you suppose, did he choose to take such drastic action tonight? With you?"

"I—I don't know. I honestly don't."

"Then we will have to wait for him to answer that for the both of us." Briathos fell silent.

The air conditioner kicked on, and I snuggled even closer to Ouriel. I was probably just imagining it, but he felt warmer to me than he had earlier in the living room. The whine of the cooling unit lulled me into a deep sleep, and it wasn't long before I began to dream…

かそかり

Ouriel lay bloody and broken on the floor of my living room. But this time, he was awake. "Rose!" he called out. "Rose, you are here. How did you find me?"

"I didn't. I just fell asleep and, poof, here you were," I rushed over to kneel next to him. "Are you all right?"

"I do not know. The pain is incredible, but it has eased much in the last half hour. Are *you* all right?"

"Yes, thanks to you. I can't believe you did that for me. It was unbelievable how you healed me like that—" I stopped short. "Why did you? Your dad says that it was unnecessary."

Ouriel tried to smile through his pain. "My father knows well how necessary it was. He is simply not pleased with his son risking his existence for anyone. Even you. I am all he has left, much like you with your sisters."

I skimmed my fingertips lightly over Ouriel's forehead, brushing his hair back, off his clammy face. My heart tripped. "Is there anything I can do to make you feel better?"

"No, my sweet. Your touch is all I need."

"But your father and Miriam both said that you don't like to be touched." I rested my head on his chest. "How is my holding you making things any better for you?"

"It is true that I do not like to be touched, Rose. Except, it seems, by you. And that, I believe, I like entirely too much for my own good," Ouriel whispered into my hair as he brushed a soft kiss across my forehead.

I was dumbfounded. I wasn't sure what he meant by that, and I was too afraid to ask. If he said something like I was the little sister he never had, I might have to shoot myself. Or get Gen to do it for me. She'd probably be glad to.

"Rose?" Ouriel sounded panicked. "Are you still with me?"

"Yes. I'm right here. And I'm not leaving." I seriously needed to put my issues aside and concentrate only on him.

"Good," he breathed. "I need you. I need you like I have never needed anyone else. And I did not realize just how much until I saw that demon trying to devour you tonight. I nearly lost focus and tore him limb from limb."

I shifted up onto my elbow so that I could gently, very gently, trace a finger down the side of his face. Could it be possible that he needed me the way I needed him? Did he understand the pain I had felt, seeing him near death tonight? Had he felt the same way when it had been me in that situation?

I couldn't believe it, but his eyes told me it was true. They burned with emotion, but rather than the ferocity I'd seen earlier, their light was now softer somehow—like a banked fire.

"Rose," Ouriel reached a hand up to cup the nape of my neck, "I am helplessly in love with you, and I do not know just how I came to be so." He dragged my head down into a blistering kiss.

Before I could respond in kind, he pulled away to look into my eyes. My breath came in ragged gasps, and the outline of his face grew hazy and clouded. I felt myself floating back up into consciousness and away from him. I reached for him, desperate to stay, but my arms closed around emptiness.

"Ouriel," I moaned.

"Rose," he called from a distance, "Rose, I am here. Wake up."

ℰᴕℰᴕ

My eyes snapped open to find Ouriel smiling sweetly at me. The color of his skin remained ashen, but his cuts and bruises had almost faded completely. He bent to kiss my forehead.

"Thank you for staying with me. I could feel your presence."

I couldn't respond. My dream had choked me with a combination of yearning and stark embarrassment. Ouriel said nothing else, so we continued to lie there in silence for quite some time before I recovered enough to remember that Briathos had been in the room with us.

"Ouriel, I forgot! Your father—"

"Is right here." Briathos stepped back into the room from just outside the doorway.

"Father!" Ouriel exclaimed with a smile, and I immediately tried to pull away from him. His iron grasp only clamped me closer to his side.

Briathos walked to the bed, sat on its edge, and scanned Ouriel's face. "How are you, my son?"

"I am nearly well now, Father, thanks to Rose." He struggled into a sitting position. "I could feel her near me, and her thoughts guided me back to myself."

"She was correct, then." Briathos pinned me with one of his piercing glares. "She insisted upon remaining by your side."

I ducked my head and pried my body away from Ouriel so neither of them could see my flaming face. I staggered across the room with the eyes of both Warriors heavy on me and fell into Gen's reading chair. I'd never been so thankful Warriors couldn't see into my mind and ferret out the scene that had just burned its image there. *Crap.* I would never be able to be in the presence of either again if they knew I had been dreaming of kissing Ouriel. I must have gone seriously insane. The guy was nearly dead, and I was making out with him mentally. I needed serious therapy—

"Rose?" Ouriel's voice broke into my mental diatribe. "What are you thinking about?"

Desperate to clear my head, I smiled to stall for time. "Um…nothing! It's…uh…just been a long night." *Think quicker, stupid!* "And I'm so relieved you're okay. I was really scared. And it's my fault that you were hurt. I'm so sorry." *Could I sound any lamer?*

"Good. I, for one, am glad you realize the idiocy of running out of your house without Warrior protection," Briathos boomed. "You nearly got my son killed."

Chastened, my head dropped and tears stung my eyes. I didn't dare look up for fear the two Warriors would see them. The possibility that I might see the same accusation in Ouriel's eyes that I had just heard in his father's words was no small burden either.

I got up to leave the room, feeling disgraced, when Ouriel snapped, "Father, I am just as much to blame for what happened as Rose is." He maneuvered to sit scowl-to-scowl with Briathos on the side of the bed. "Do not unleash your temper upon her. If you wish to vent on someone, it will be me."

Shocked, I peeped at Briathos in order to gauge his reaction, but his eyes were doing battle with his son's. Neither Warrior broke contact as Briathos bit out, "Rose, will you excuse us now? I must have a private word with my son."

"She does not need to leave, Father. Whatever needs to be said about her henceforth will be said in her presence!"

"Ouriel, really—I'd rather go. It's okay." I didn't want to be around either Warrior at the moment. "Um— Briathos, sir, I *am* sorry for endangering myself purposely. It will not happen again." Unable to say anything else, I ran out of the room as fast as my pride allowed me.

Behind me, I heard one of the Warriors, probably Briathos, walk across the room and close the door. I fled for the relative refuge that was my bedroom, but I wouldn't enjoy any peace there either. My sisters accosted me before I could even get my door closed.

Miriam crushed me to her in a tight hug. "You scared us to death!" She ran her hands up and down my arms and back, as if she didn't believe I was completely healed. She pulled away slightly and shook me a bit. "Don't you ever do that again!"

"Seriously, Rose, I will kick your butt if I have to," Gen joined in. "You scared the hell out of me."

I didn't know what to say. I knew my sisters loved me, but sometimes it was easy to forget just how much. I looked at both of them and the tears that had been threatening since I woke in Gen's room gushed out. Bawling like the child I claimed not to be, I sank down onto my bed and covered my face with my hands.

Miriam put her arm around my shoulders and drew me close again. "Rose, sweetie, it's going to be okay, really."

I still couldn't speak. It had all become too much for me to bear. I'd had no one to confide in for far too long. I also didn't think either of my sisters could possibly understand what was really wrong with me. I was devastated by what had happened tonight to both Ouriel and me. Not to mention that I was still dealing with Ishmael's absence and Javi's death. I was also going to be living in terror of demons for the foreseeable future. *I don't even know how to feel about that last little detail.* The concept that I was desirable to the demon hordes was as inane as it was bloodcurdling.

But none of that overwhelmed me as much as the discovery of the depths of my feelings for Ouriel. I had fallen in love with a Warrior who could never love me the way I needed him to.

I also hadn't forgotten the fact that he was nearly 2,000 years older than I was.

The whole situation tortured me. I wasn't one of those girls who had gone boy crazy at puberty. I had noticed members of the opposite sex, but they'd never really interested me. It was true to my style that the first male to ever engage my emotions would have to be a Warrior. I never could do anything the smart way. Not only would Ouriel never notice me, but relationships between Warriors and Guardians were frowned upon. I was beyond stupid.

Shaken by my sudden onslaught of tears, Gen asked, "What's wrong, honey? Is Ouri okay? He's not—he's not—" Her voice broke before I could interrupt.

"Ouriel is fine, thanks be to God," I said as Gen's fears broke apart my self-pity. "He just woke up, and now he and Briathos are in your room arguing."

Gen glanced in the direction of her room. "Two angry Warriors in there? I hope they don't break anything!"

"They're arguing?" Disbelief rang in Miriam's voice. "About what? I've never seen them so much as get irritated with one another."

"It's all my fault." That was quickly becoming my mantra. "Briathos blames me for nearly killing Ouriel, and Ouriel says it was all his fault. And I don't know—I just can't take any more of this! It's all making me crazy," I finished on the verge of hysteria.

"Rose, you've been through a lot recently," Miriam soothed. "It's hard, I know, but you can't lose control now. It's okay to cry and feel like you can't go on, but know that you must and you will."

"She's right, Rose." Gen joined us on the bed. "The path of a Guardian, Sightless or not, is never an easy one. We all carry heavy burdens. And it seems you are not going to be an exception to that, as much as Miriam and I wish we could spare you."

Gen surprised me by putting her arms around me, too. It had been so long since she and I had touched, much less talked—really talked—to each other, that her kindness caused another chorus of sobs to erupt from me. Comforting words from Miriam were common and, therefore, too often taken for granted. Gen, on the other hand, rarely ever touched me. We had never gotten along well because the nature of her Gift naturally made it difficult for her to relate to other humans, even her own sisters.

I studied her tired face. It was amazing how, even while living in the same house, it was all too easy to ignore another human being. For the first time, I noticed that Gen was no longer the carefree teenager I had followed around and idolized as a young child. Up close, I could see there were dark blue smudges under her golden brown eyes, and she looked worn down. Tonight, she looked older than Miriam.

Without thinking, I reached out, grabbed Gen in a hug, and whispered, "I love you, Jamale Genevieve." I pulled away to look back at my other sister. "I love you too, Miriam. I love both of you so much. And I don't know if I've said it enough lately."

"We love you too, Rose." Gen ran a delicate hand across my forehead and brushed my hair back behind my ear. "Never forget that."

I thought I saw tears forming in Gen's eyes, which would have been strange indeed. Before I could look closer, I heard footsteps on the wooden floor in the hallway. All three of us turned as Ouriel filled my doorway.

"Oh! I am sorry." He fidgeted, shifting from side to side. "I did not mean to interrupt. I will return to speak with Rose when you have finished."

"No." Miriam stood. "I think we are finished. Gen and I will go to speak with your father in the kitchen. Maybe you both should meet us there when you're done."

Miriam and Gen moved quickly out of my room, leaving me alone with the one being in the world whose presence I craved almost as much as Ishmael's.

CHAPTER 7

Ouriel stood, silent and framed by the doorway of my bedroom while I struggled not to show any hint of the mortification, desire, and regret roiling within me. He looked his usual distant self as he stepped into my room and closed the door. He hesitated for only a moment before crossing the gap between us. My bed dipped as he sank down next to me.

We sat there for a minute or so, looking anywhere but at each other, and I found myself regretting that I didn't spent more of my time cleaning the environmental hazard I called a bedroom.

Ouriel broke the silence. "I am sorry for what I said to you earlier. It was horribly wrong of me, and I beg your forgiveness."

I shook my head. "No, Ouriel. It's my fault. I really shouldn't have yelled at you, and I seriously should not have run out of the house like that. I'm really sorry. I just didn't think that I was really in danger. I am *so* sorry."

That was sad. Could I have possibly used *more* adverbs in a single apology?

He raked his hands through his hair. "You need not apologize to me. I treated you poorly this afternoon and without good reason. I should never have said some of those things to you."

"Ouriel, stop. It's okay." I grabbed for his wrists, and he surprised me by allowing my touch. When he grasped my hand in his, all rational thought evaporated, and I couldn't remember what I'd wanted to say next.

"Are you sure?" Ouriel tightened his hold on me. "Because the truth is I never wish to be rid of you. I do not care to even think about spending a day not in your company."

Struck dumb by his words and distracted by the heat radiating from where he was touching me, I couldn't form a coherent reply. The ability to breathe escaped me when Ouriel pulled me close.

"You are the bravest, kindest, most humble being I have ever had the good fortune to meet, Rose, and you frighten me terribly. You see, I have not allowed myself to come to care for anyone new since the death of my mother quite some time ago. However, *you* have somehow breached all my defenses, and now I care entirely too much for you. I care more than I believed it possible to care for anyone other than the remaining members of my own family."

Ouriel paused and waited expectantly for me to reply. I didn't know how to answer him without sounding entirely stupid, so I sat in silence, waiting for him to go on.

"Rose, I am not very affectionate, nor do I have the ability to express my emotions well. I am sure you have noticed this." He beamed me a grin I couldn't help but return.

"Not really," I quipped, relaxed by his smile. "It must not be too obvious that you are aloof, outwardly cold, and very intimidating."

He rewarded my sarcasm with a rare chuckle. "You have a way about you that speaks to my very soul. It frightens me, and I feel my attachment to you has grown much too strong, too quickly." His face twisted with worry. "In fact, it is that detail about which my father wanted to speak to me earlier. He believes I am allowing my personal feelings for you to interfere with my role as your protector. Unfortunately, I cannot help but agree with him. His suggestion is that I step back from the role and allow him to take over."

"No!" My stomach turned at the idea of traveling anywhere without Ouriel. I fought for control and then continued more quietly, "You can't do that. I need you."

For once, Ouriel's steely restraint slipped. His dark blue eyes found mine, and I was struck by the despair I saw in them. I noticed, too, a flicker of hope beginning to catch hold in their depths. "You would be safer with him. His feelings toward you would not interfere with—"

"*Feelings*? Just what are these feelings of yours that are so overwhelming?"

"Surely you must know!"

"No I don't, Ouriel. I barely understand how I feel about you! Do you really expect me to guess what's in that mystifying brain of yours? It's impossible!"

If he was trying to tell me his feelings for me were out of control, I was not the type of girl to assume he meant it in any kind of romantic way. He was going to have to state his emotions clearly. I would not deceive myself into presuming anything more than friendship might ever exist between us.

"As I said earlier, this is not easy for me. You have no problems coming to terms with your emotions and expressing them. I am severely handicapped in that area." Ouriel looked as though he were ransacking his brain for the correct verbiage. "I am trying to explain to you that I feel much more for you than a protector should."

"So does Ishmael. He loves me like his daughter and that never seemed to be a problem for anyone."

"I feel much more for you than even that," Ouriel responded softly. "Which is why I should leave you to my father's protection."

My mind raced. I was pretty sure I finally understood, positively, what Ouriel was trying to get across to me.

"Ouriel, are you saying you—like—are in love with me or something?" *Crap. I seriously should not be allowed to speak to members of the opposite sex.*

"Yes! Is it not obvious?" Ouriel snapped. I chose not to interject and point out how *un*loving he sounded just then. "I love you more than I had ever thought it possible to love anyone. I have loved you at least since the moment I saw you go after that demoness to protect Ishmael. You are beautiful, brilliant, amazing. How could I not be completely lost to you?"

What could I say in return to such a declaration? Rather than try, I climbed into Ouriel's lap. His body tensed for only a moment before he reached around and crushed me to him. I wound my arms around his neck and rested my head on his shoulder. I didn't even try to suppress the laughter that fizzed up within me and rang out into the room. When I pulled back to look up at him, he seemed a little confused by my reaction to his declaration of love.

"Oh, sorry! I guess now is the time I should say that I kind of like you, too." I aimed a teasing grin at him. "So, where do we go from here?"

Ouriel stilled. "What do you mean?"

"I mean, what do we do now? How are we supposed to, you know, go forward from here? With us?"

"There is so much I wish I could say—so much wish I could tell you—" He broke off to wipe a hand across his face. "But I cannot. Please, just believe me when I say that it would be reckless for either of us to lose sight of the need for your immediate protection and education. You need both of those to survive what lies ahead, and I cannot allow anything to distract from either. Not even me."

Ouriel's words tore at my heart. Livid, I slid off his lap and back onto my bed. "Fine. By all means, let's put our feelings aside and focus on our duty. War and danger are much more important than something as frivolous as two people falling in love."

Ouriel reached for me again. I shrugged his hand off my shoulder and stood.

Heedless of my mood, he leaped up to join me. "That is not what I meant! Please, listen to me. Your safety must be my top priority right now. Can you not imagine what losing you would do to me? I could not bear it!"

"I'm sure that's true, Ouriel, but you can't tell me that your father hasn't influenced this decision of yours at all."

"He has not. Believe me, I would be with you, this moment, if I—"

"And I'm sure your father would have a lot more to say on the subject. It's not just that a relationship might endanger me, but he would also probably be adamant about you not becoming involved with a human, Guardian or not."

"That is not true either. My father does not control my decision making in this matter. I have no care for anyone's preconceived notions on Warrior-Guardian relationships. I *do* care, however, that we survive the coming weeks!"

His words sucked the all the fury out of my zeppelin of anger. It was pointless to argue any further with Ouriel while I lived in the shadows of such imminent danger. At least he seemed to be planning some kind of path for us to be together in the future. Sighing, I decided to let the whole thing go—for now.

What other choice did I have?

"All right, Ouri. I'll wait—but only on one condition."

"Name it."

"You remain my protector. Your father may follow along if he wants to, but I will not submit to anyone but you watching over me."

"Rose—"

"You or no one, Ouriel. I mean it."

The Warrior glared at me for a moment. I saw both worry and anger in his eyes. I watched those emotions escape his control long enough to creep across his face before he shackled them once more into the dungeon of his mind.

"Fine." He scowled. "I will remain as your protector. God knows that I would die to keep you safe. I only hope it will be enough."

That statement struck a painful chord in my chest. I didn't like the idea that he may have to lose his life to save anyone else's, especially mine. *Crap.* Now he had me doubting whether or not I wanted him as my protector. *Well, two can play the guilt-trip game!*

"I would willingly lay down my life for you, too."

Ouriel snagged me into a suffocating hug. "You will do no such thing," he groaned into my hair. "I forbid it!"

"If you're going to love me—" I struggled to get the breathless words out, "—you need to learn that you can never forbid me anything. I will do as I see fit. Just as you will. Never forget that."

He pulled back and hoisted me up to his height, so he could stare directly into my eyes. "You will not die. I will see to it."

I was shocked into silence by the fear I saw in him. My only answer was a shiver when he allowed my body to slide down the length of his and land shakily on the floor.

"I won't die, Ouriel. Not with you protecting me." I ran my hand through the long, beautiful hair that had long since fallen from his ponytail. We remained there for a few moments before he stepped away.

"Rose, come. I think it is time we join the conversation in the kitchen."

I followed him down the hall, past the living room and den, into my kitchen. Miriam, Gen, Shadrach, and Briathos were all there, engaged in a rather heated conversation. Miriam stood at the sink, staring out the window into the backyard, her back stiff and unyielding. The other three sat at the breakfast table. Gen's golden brown hair glistened under the fluorescent light as she nodded at something Shad was saying. He and Briathos faced away from Ouriel and me.

Ouriel caught my hand in his just before every set of eyes in the room slammed into us. I looked up at him, and he spared me a reassuring glance before facing our relatives. Because of her position, only Gen had seen the small exchange between the two of us. Her eyes narrowed, and her mouth pressed into a tight line.

Briathos and Shadrach remained silent in response to our arrival, but Miriam rushed over. "Ouri, you really should sit down. I know you're almost entirely healed, but you still shouldn't overdo."

"I am fine. Thank you for your concern, Miriam, but I wish to remain standing." Ouriel turned to his father. "Sir, I have—I mean to say—*Rose* and I have come to a decision."

Ouriel squeezed my hand, and his father cut in, "I am sure it is a sensible one, my son."

"It is," Ouriel retorted. "Very sensible, indeed. Rose and I discussed, at length, her options for protection in the near future. Together, we reached the conclusion that it is in her best interest to remain under my protection and tutelage."

Everyone in the room turned, as if watching a Ping-Pong match, to see Briathos' reaction to his son's statement. I had no idea what Briathos had said to Ouriel and my family during my absence, but I assumed it had been something to do with separating us.

I would not allow that to happen.

No matter how scary Briathos could be.

Intent on a seething Briathos, I nearly missed Gen stand. She walked across the kitchen, and, when she reached Ouri, Miriam, and me, she turned and assumed a power I rarely saw her use. "I completely agree. Now, if you all will excuse me, there is an entity that requires attention waiting in my room." With that, she swept out of the room in a way only someone as beautiful and self-assured as Gen could. No one else noticed that she brushed the back of my hand with hers as she passed by me.

"This is absurd," Briathos fumed. "Ouriel, we have already discussed this matter in private, and I do not believe you would wish to do so again with an audience."

"Father, as I said, Rose and I have made this decision together. I will not recant. Neither will she."

"Ouriel, listen to reason! You are allowing your emotions to overrule your intellect when it comes to this girl!"

"Father, I submit it is your judgment that has become clouded with your own fear of losing me," Ouriel murmured.

Briathos shot out of his seat and made for Ouriel, but Shadrach bounded between them. Briathos glowed a darker shade of amber than I had seen on any Warrior before.

"How dare you?" he choked out. "I have sent you into battle more times than I care to count and never once flinched!"

"Maybe it is not to battle that you fear losing me."

"Ouriel!" Briathos bellowed. "You must remember who this girl is! Remember your sacred duty!"

Shocked, my face burned with shame. Everyone turned to look at me, and they all had pity in their eyes. All of them but Ouriel. The sweet expression on his face caused me to jut out my chin in defiance.

"Briathos, sir—" I was desperate not to hyperventilate. "—you have my respect as a great Warrior and as Ouriel's father. However, I refuse to be insulted in my own kitchen. I realize a Sightless human of Guardian descent is not worthy of your son's life or protection. I will in no way contradict that. I will, though, refuse to be separated from him. And *that* you will learn to deal with."

Briathos at least looked embarrassed. "Young lady, you grossly misunderstand me!"

I swallowed hard. "I don't think I do."

"Briathos," Miriam interrupted, "you must remember that Rose has very little Guardian training."

"Yes," Shad added, looking eager to direct the conversation away from more dangerous waters. "And Ouriel is working quickly to remedy that. Right, Ouri?"

"Yes. And, Father, you may rest assured I will never forget my sacred duty. It is more impossible now than ever."

I started to ask what all the talk of "sacred duty" meant when Shadrach said, "May I make a suggestion that might please both of you?"

"Certainly," father and son chorused.

"I believe the coalition working the perimeter of Rose's school could do with further reinforcement. So, to table any further debate, I propose you join us there, Briathos, and help us to secure the area daily. That would allow you to be close at hand, while Ouriel could then remain in even closer proximity to Rose inside the school."

I tried not to groan out loud. I didn't want this older, even crankier version of Ouriel hanging over my every minute at school. Then a thought struck me. "Wait a second, Shad. You're working outside my school too? How many of you guys are there?"

Shad looked like he'd swallowed a thumbtack. "Uh—you don't need to worry about that. Ouriel has done a thorough job of ensuring no demon will be able to repeat either of the attacks that have occurred there recently."

"But it's not right!" I knew I would never win this argument, but I couldn't help railing against anyone risking his or her life for mine. "Why are all these people endangering themselves for me? It's stupid. I'm a Sightless human who happens to have had Guardian parents." I wrenched my hand from Ouriel's and threw myself down in one of the kitchen chairs. "Why, all of a sudden, have I become so important?"

My outburst was met with total silence. Anger and fear for those who had volunteered to protect me was a heavier burden than I wanted to carry.

Miriam placed her hand on my shoulder. "You are, and have always been, important to this family. I know that doesn't help you understand why you are suddenly so sought after by demons, but that's something I can't explain either. Right now, keeping you safe is our main goal. Shad and Briathos will be there mostly to make sure others are not in danger. After Javi, we have to be more careful. We never did find out how that demon got through. I'm beginning to think we may have a leak somewhere."

"If that's true, Miri, then it's getting too dangerous."
I sighed. "Maybe I should just quit school altogether. I
seem to be a catastrophe magnet."

"No!" Miriam's voice felt like a slap to the face. "If
you're going to have any chance at a normal life, you
have to graduate. You're almost done."

"I could do an online—"

"I said no! More than anything, you've always wanted a normal human life. I will not let that be taken from
you." She sent me a pointed glare. "Do you understand
me?"

I nodded and gave her a weak smile. I didn't want
her to be more upset than she already was. "I understand,
Miriam. I just don't want any of you hurt because of me.
I couldn't stand it!"

"I know, baby, but *we* couldn't stand it if something
happened to *you*, so you'll just have to deal with it." Miriam dropped a kiss on the top of my head. "Now, I think
we'd all best be getting to bed. We've had a long day and
need to get up early in the morning."

"Yes. Ouriel and I should leave you until morning."
Briathos sent his son a pointed look.

"Thank you, again, Ouriel, for saving my baby sister.
I am eternally in your debt." Miriam laid a soft hand on
his cheek. He flinched only a little, and I smothered a
grin.

"Come on, Miriam. Let's get to bed." Shadrach rescued Ouriel by reaching for Miriam's hand and pulling
her towards the hallway.

The two Warriors and I watched the couple walk out of the room, hand in hand, whispering to one another. I was sure all three of us were hit with the same intense yearning. The intimacy that was so obvious between my sister and brother-in-law was almost painful for the lonely to witness.

Briathos breathed out on a sigh. "Come, Ouriel. Let us leave Rose to her rest."

"Father, I will follow you in a moment. Rose and I must discuss our plans for tomorrow before I leave. We've lost out on an entire night's work."

Briathos grimaced. He obviously didn't want to leave us alone but couldn't seem to come up with an alternative. "Very well. Do as you must. Good night, Rose. It has been an honor to finally meet you. Ouriel, I expect you to follow me in no more than ten minutes. We have plans to discuss as well." The words had only just left his mouth when Briathos disintegrated.

"I would say your first meeting with my father went well," Ouriel drawled from behind me. I turned and attempted to pin him with my most vicious stare, but he only grinned in response. "It was not nearly as bad as I would have expected. He is typically much more gruff and condescending. Too many years in command, you see."

"You mean he's usually worse than that?"

"Yes, but I often do not notice and have heard many say I can be far worse."

"Seriously?" I shook my head in disgust. "That's got to be impossible!"

"I do not know. You had a taste of my temper this afternoon." Ouriel twisted a lock of my hair through his fingers. "But I do seem to behave myself a bit more when you're nearby. I guess that is just one of the many harsh characteristics you seem able to soften in me." He bent to press a kiss to my forehead.

"Ouriel," I whispered, leaning into him.

He wrenched himself out of my embrace. "Rose! You will be the death of me. How am I supposed to control myself when you say my name like that? I may not be human, but I do share some of your weaknesses."

I reached for him again. "Maybe I don't want you to control yourself."

"But I must!" He ducked out of my grasp. "Our lives depend on it."

His words hit me like a splash of cold water, and I could see the truth in them, even if I didn't like it.

"You're right. I'm sorry. I've just…" I trailed off. I didn't know how to say what I felt. I didn't have much experience with anything remotely romantic. "I—I've never felt like this before."

"Neither have I, Rose. That is why I wish to savor every bit of it later, when we do not have the ever present specter of battle hanging over us."

"You're right. I'll try to behave." I wrestled my hormones into submission. "What plans do we have for tomorrow?"

Ouriel grew serious. As I became more familiar and confident with him, it was easier to translate the subtle play of expressions across his handsome face. "We will arrive for school at the usual time, and, tomorrow evening, we will spend an extra two hours on your training making up for what we have missed tonight. You will be learning more about Guardian traditions, and I hope you will also have chosen a weapon by the end of our session."

"You don't waste time do you?" I grumbled. "Well, teach me at your own risk. Let's pray I don't do either of us irreparable damage tomorrow night."

"I am sure you will. However, I will see you first thing in the morning anyway, my sweet." Ouriel bent to kiss me on the forehead one last time before dissolving just as his father had only minutes before.

CHAPTER 8

I woke up the next morning with a smile and one single, overwhelming thought—Ouriel loved me. He was actually *in* love with me. I couldn't believe it. It didn't seem possible that he could feel that way about me, but Ouriel was not someone to say—much less feel—things lightly. That made the whole thing seem even more miraculous to me. Even though guilt for Ishmael and Javier tried to push in on my ecstatic mood, I shoved it away. I decided that, this once, I could give myself permission to feel happy. *Just for today, I refuse to believe that all the evil in the world is my fault.*

I practically floated down the hall on my way to shower and continued in the same way until I sat, waiting, for Ouriel to Jump into our front hallway. I was suddenly attacked by a bout of nerves. Did I look okay? Was my hair in place? Should I actually put on some makeup?

I was about to rush back to the bathroom when Ouricl himself appeared.

He was dressed in his schoolboy uniform and had his hair tied back again. He also carried a box in addition to his backpack. Although we both tried to act as naturally as possible, neither of us could resist the temptation of avoiding direct eye contact.

I sneaked a peek at Ouriel, who had assumed a nervous stance. The idiocy of the situation compelled me to break the awkward silence. "So…uh…what's in the case?" I wasn't sure I even wanted to know, but I *had* to say something.

"Makeup," Ouriel responded, clearly relieved that I had broken the ice, but I was struck dumb. I resisted the urge to run to the nearest mirror and check my reflection. *Do I look* that *bad*? "It is to recreate the wound on the side of your face. Its sudden disappearance might be noticed by those charming Sightless girls in your classes."

Duh! "Oh, I hadn't realized…" I reached up to where I'd had a scar forming just yesterday. The skin was smooth and utterly perfect. "Well, I guess I need to thank you for that, too. I'm just vain enough to be relieved I won't have a scar there for the rest of my life. So who's going to do the honors?" I could barely put mascara on without stabbing my eyeball, so I knew it couldn't be me. Makeup application was not one of my talents.

Ouriel looked shocked I'd even asked. "Genevieve, of course. She is an excellent makeup artist."

"Oh, right. I knew that." Did I? Truthfully, I hadn't paid Gen much attention in the last few years. Our relationship had been strained since I hit puberty. I wasn't sure how it had happened. I preferred to blame Gen by claiming she had abandoned me when I became a difficult teenager. Looking back, though, I realized it might not have been entirely her fault. Maybe I had shut her out.

"Come, Rose, we must hurry." Ouriel pushed me down the hall toward Gen's room. "Take the case and wake her if you must, but be quick about it."

I knocked on Gen's door, and she answered with a muffled, "Come in."

I opened the door to find her crawling out of bed. She didn't look nearly awake enough to be bothered.

"Um…Gen? Can you do me a favor?" I hated asking anyone for anything.

"What is it, Rose?" she answered, not too grouchily.

"I need my cut back. When Ouriel healed me last night, it disappeared along with my other injuries, and, well, some of the kids at school might notice that it's gone. Can you do it for me? I wouldn't ask except that Ouriel told me you were the best at it."

"Of course I'll do it," Gen huffed. "Sit in my chair, and I'll be right back. I need to go to the bathroom."

I sat dutifully and looked around Gen's room while waiting for her to return. For the first time, I noticed that she had only three pictures on the walls. One was of our parents on their wedding day. The second was of all five of us together, taken just before my parents died, and the last was one of Gen holding me as a baby.

She was probably only ten when that last picture was taken, and she looked so happy, staring down at me, while my baby-self reached a chubby little hand toward her face. I remembered the picture from my earliest childhood but hadn't seen it in years. Something in it made a piece of me feel broken.

I shook off the feeling when Gen trudged back into the room. She made quick work of fixing me up to look wounded, stitches and all. When she handed me a mirror, I was shocked by how real it appeared.

"Holy crap, Gen! You're good."

"I know." She laughed and patted me on the head. "Now get out of here and go to school."

"Okay. Love you!" I bounded up, kissed Gen, and ran down the hall to find Ouriel waiting for me with something in his hand. "What's that?" My earlier anxiety seemed to have dissipated altogether.

"It is a gift." Ouriel flushed orange. "I made it for you, and I expect you to carry it at all times."

Flattered, I looked more closely at the object he held out to me and realized it was a smaller version of the Bowie knife Ouriel had taken to carrying in his backpack.

"I don't know what to say. It's beautiful. And only a *little* scary." I reached for the bundle. Its sheath was a soft and supple black leather attached to a belt of some sort. Intertwined roses were stamped into the entire length of it. I slid out the knife with a whispered swoosh and found the same pattern etched into the hilt and down the center of the blade. It felt good and balanced in my hand.

"You made this?"

He couldn't quite meet my gaze. "Yes, I make all of my own weapons."

"You really are amazing. Thank you so much!" I hugged my Warrior—the one who hated to be touched— and was happily surprised to note that I was the first to pull away. "Now, how exactly am I supposed to wear this?" I held the tangled mess up to him.

"I made the harness and sheath to fit around your waist and conceal the bulk of the knife. It will lie flat against the small of your back horizontally so that your blouse, and most other shirts, will camouflage it well. Make sure that the blade always points to the left so you can grasp the hilt easily with your right hand."

I fiddled with it for a moment but couldn't seem to unknot the straps of leather. I finally gave up, knowing I would embarrass myself with what I had to say next.

"Um—can you help me? I can't seem to do this right," I mumbled.

Ouriel looked as if he was going to bolt for only a split second when I lifted the hem of my sailor blouse to expose my midriff. I had to admit he was making progress when he took the knife from me and strapped it to my body. He didn't allow one cell of his skin to touch mine. And he blew out a pent up breath when I let down my shirt.

The weight of the knife against my back was oddly comforting. A smile made its way across my face. For the first time in my life, I felt somewhat capable of defending myself. My safety had finally become my own responsi-

bility—at least partly and it was downright empower-
ing.

I grabbed him in another hug. "Thank you, Ouri." I
planted a shy peck on his cheek. "But I hope I never need
to use it."

"As much as I hope the same, I fear that is impossible." He sighed. "Come now, let us go. Are you ready?"

"Yes, are *you*?"

"Yes," he answered with a self-deprecating grin.
"And try not to be so pleased with yourself about my reaction to your touch. I believe I am finally growing accustomed to it."

Yeah right, I thought. I wrapped myself around him
in preparation for the Jump and smothered a giggle when
he sucked in his breath. My self-satisfaction didn't last
long. His strong arms crushed me to his body, and I suffered the same reaction he did.

We reappeared behind my new favorite dumpster at
school, both gasping for air. Boasting aside, I was pretty
sure that both of us felt like we'd been run over by a
semi-truck.

We pried ourselves apart and tried to regain our
composure. "I—um—I'll see you in class," I stammered
as I staggered towards the building.

"Yes," was all I heard him say as I tripped gracefully
over a parking curb.

‿✺‿

Only one incident stood out in my day. It took place in the cafeteria at lunch—involving Ana, of course, and her never-ending attempt to gain Ouriel's attention.

He and I had thwarted her previous efforts all morning by remaining close together, but we'd had to separate for a few moments when I ran to the bathroom to wash my hands before getting into the lunch line.

When I returned, I found Ana standing in front of Ouriel. He resembled a cheetah that had been cornered by a gazelle. I fought back a laugh at the ridiculous notion, until she sidled even closer to him, put one hand on his shoulder, the other on his stomach, and stood on tiptoe to whisper something in his ear.

Ouriel's eyes flashed to mine, and a tidal wave of fury slashed through my body. I strode toward them, but Ana did not see my approach. Her back was to me. Ouriel blanched as he sensed the anger ripping off me. I didn't care. I was too busy fighting the urge to grab Ana by the hair and rip her off of my Warrior.

Sadly, Ouriel elbowed her aside before I had the pleasure of doing it for him.

"Hello, Ana." A polite chill formed icicles on my words.

"Rose! Uh—hello." For once, Ana looked nervous and embarrassed. Her gaze darted back and forth between Ouriel and me.

"I regret that I must decline your invitation yet again, Ana, but—as you can see—I already have a lunch partner." Ouriel reached for my hand and pulled me to his side. "I would also appreciate your restraint in touching me again in future. I do not care for unwelcome advances."

Ouriel draped his arm—and our still intertwined hands—across my shoulders and ushered me into the line for food. I risked a glance back at Ana. Her face was mottled with anger, and something akin to hatred coalesced in her eyes as she watched us pick up our plastic sporks. The look on her face made me feel sick to my stomach.

I clung even tighter to Ouriel's steadying hand and leaned into him. "I think we've made an enemy."

"Then she will be one of the least dangerous I have faced," he said, dismissing my concern. "I regret being so curt with her, but I can See the malevolent feelings she harbors for you."

"I know she hates me, but I've never been able to figure out why. I've never done anything to her."

"It's easy to guess," a timid voice behind me whispered.

I turned around to find it came from Taylor, the quiet girl from our first period class with Mrs. Palmer. I had noticed her a few times in class. She rarely spoke, unless given the opportunity to read out loud—a task she reveled in. I'd often thought she was a pretty girl—with her big brown doe eyes and long curly blonde hair—and that she would have run with Ana's crowd, if she hadn't been so shy.

"What's easy to guess?" I wasn't sure Taylor was even speaking to me.

"Don't you see?" She blushed bright red. "She's jealous of you."

"*What*? Why should she be jealous of me?" I laughed at the ludicrous notion. Ouriel and Taylor shared a glance, and I thought I caught the beginnings of an eye-roll in Taylor's expression before she turned away. "Seriously! I mean, look at the girl! I know I'm not ugly or anything, but I could never compete with her. She's like rock star gorgeous."

"Rose, you consistently underestimate yourself." Ouriel sounded exasperated.

One by one, the three of us ordered, paid the cashier, and picked up our lunch trays. There was an awkward moment when Taylor made to follow us to my usual table but paused, blushed again, and turned the other way.

"Taylor, would you care to sit with Rose and me?" Ouriel asked, stopping her before she had gotten more than a few steps away. "We would not mind."

"Really?" Taylor's face lit up. "I would love to."

I smiled to myself. Ouriel was uncomfortable around people he didn't know well, but he couldn't allow anyone else to suffer for it.

ତଽତଽତ

The last bell rang, and Ouriel and I met in our new spot for the jump home. Most of our day had been peaceful and the lunch with Taylor had gained us each a new friend. I really liked her. She was shy but smart and honest, and I found myself looking forward to seeing her the next day. It was a new and strange feeling. I'd never had the luxury of being able to socialize outside my family, much less Guardian, circles.

Ouriel and I arrived at my house short of breath, as always. I wasn't sure I was ever going to get over the nerves and excitement I felt around him.

"You must change into more comfortable clothing. We will be doing some physical training before we begin our academic study," Ouriel tossed over his shoulder as he headed to the bathroom. He carried a bag he must have stashed in the living room while he was waiting for me earlier that morning.

I ran to my own room and pulled on some shorts and a tank top. I also grabbed some socks and my tennis shoes. When I was done, I met Ouriel in the hallway just as he was coming out of the bathroom. His hair was down again and he had on black sweatpants with white stripes running down the outside seam and a white T-shirt with cut off sleeves. It really wasn't fair how good he looked in anything he put on. He was wearing tennis shoes too, and that set me to worrying about just how "physical" this training was going to be.

Ouriel took a moment to look over my change in uniform. His eyes lingered on the darkly tanned expanse of leg my shorts had left exposed, and he blew out a harsh breath. I had to fight a blush when he looked up at me and grinned.

"It seems I am becoming much more accustomed to your presence. And I believe that I am going to thoroughly enjoy the continuing process." Before I could respond, he shifted topics. "Today, we are going to begin with a short run and some conditioning exercises. Then we will work to familiarize you with a typical Guardian arsenal and possibly choose a weapon for you."

I groaned. I really hated running. It wasn't something that I ever enjoyed, even though I was decent at it. My Gym teacher had repeatedly tried to get me to join the track or cross country teams, saying that I had the potential to be an excellent runner. The problem was, it bored me. Not that I didn't envy the people who could run, like my sisters, with speed and grace. I just totally lacked the determination necessary to force myself to suffer through it.

"I believe your family has a fully equipped gym. Have you ever used it?"

"Sometimes. It's built underneath the house. It has no doors or windows, so I have to get Miriam or Gen to Jump me in if I want to go down there."

"Yes. I have always found it interesting that Guardian families must ensure their younger members are kept from their weapons and such because they cannot be trusted to restrain themselves from playing with them."

"Of course, Ouriel, because we lowly Guardians are born with actual children's minds, instead of the fully matured ones you Warriors have at birth."

"I have often pitied the human state of ignorance in infancy." Ouriel laughed. "Now come nearer, so that we may Jump to the gym."

I stepped into his arms, and we instantly melted away. I reached up to run my fingers through his hair as we re-formed in the gym below. Ouriel stroked both sides of my face with his hands and brought his forehead to rest on mine.

"I cannot tell you how you have touched my life, Rose. For the first time in centuries, the sucking void within me seems to have abated." Ouriel shook as he spoke.

"Good." I rested my cheek against his chest. There simply were no other words in my head.

Ouriel molded my body to his for just a moment before he released me and stepped away. "All right, it is time for what I am sure will become your favorite part of our new daily schedule—a run." His voice held the hint of a snicker.

"Oh yes. It's my favorite thing to do on any afternoon. I am *so* thankful that Miriam and Shadrach have kept the gym up to date and that there are *two* treadmills," I threw back. "I really would hate to have you watch me wheeze and groan through a run. My self-esteem would never recover."

"I am sure it would not. But I am resolved to like you, nonetheless, and I am only forcing you to run one mile today. Even you should be able to make it that far without completely embarrassing yourself."

I stuck my tongue out at his back as he led the way to our state-of-the-art treadmills. He paused to stretch for only a moment, hopped on, and was at an all-out sprint in less than thirty seconds.

I took my time stretching so I could watch the Warrior in his element. True to his nature, Ouriel was perfection in every move.

"Quit procrastinating," he called without breaking stride. The Warrior showed no signs of slowing.

Begrudgingly, I got on my treadmill and started out at a warm up pace that was barely more than a fast walk. Ouriel allowed me to remain at that speed for about a minute before reaching over and bumping my rate up by one mile an hour. At the new speed, it took me only 10 minutes to reach a mile. I slowed the treadmill to cool down, and Ouriel did the same. Of course, he'd run three miles in the same time and hadn't even broken a sweat. It was rather sickening, but then again, he did have a supernatural advantage.

"Okay," I puffed and wiped the sweat from my forehead, "what next?"

"Crunches and pushups. You are to do one hundred of the first and forty of the second—in the male form, not the female."

I smiled. These were things I was good at and actually enjoyed. Ouriel held down my feet as I whipped out two hundred crunches without stopping. Then, I rolled over and did fifty pushups, while he pumped out a countless number of his own in the same amount of time. I took my turn holding his legs while he numbered off his sit-ups.

"I am happy to see that you are proficient in some sort of physical fitness. It is promising," he blew out at the height of a sit up. I fought, unsuccessfully, the desire to stick my tongue out at him again as he disappeared behind his knees. When he finished his repetitions, he hopped up from the mat. "Now, let us see if there is a particular weapon for which you may have an aptitude."

We walked over to a storage room set in one corner of the gym, and I remembered we needed the key to it, which Miriam kept upstairs.

"Ouriel, wait. We need the key. It's in a drawer in the kitchen."

"Not necessary," he replied, placing his hand on the doorknob. To my surprise, it popped right open. He wiggled his eyebrows at me. "That is one of my lesser known talents."

I couldn't help laughing at his silly boast. It was an unexpected joy to be allowed to see beyond the harsh exterior he presented to most of the world. I adored the kindness and ridiculous sense of humor he usually kept to himself. If I thought I had loved him yesterday for his integrity and ferocity, I felt even more for him now.

"How much do you know about Guardian weaponry?" His question shook me out of my reverie.

"Uh…we use quieter weapons that cut, mostly swords or bows and arrows."

"Correct. Why do you use those rather than, say, guns?"

"Well, Guardians can't kill demons, but we can damage them, maybe even permanently. Guns make far too much noise for the limited damage they inflict on demons and expose us to the outside world too easily. The other two weapons, especially the sword, are relatively silent and can cause greater lasting damage," I answered, hoping I didn't sound too ignorant.

"Yes. Now, what you may not know is that all Guardian weapons are Warrior-made. Guardians prefer the simpler weapons of the past because there is less chance for technical malfunction, and they either require no ammunition or ammunition that can be reused. Of course, Warriors always use a blade. Do you know why?"

"Because the only way to kill a demon is to behead it. Then a Warrior is required to set the body on fire with the touch of his or her hand. You can't just set a demon on fire or just chop its head off. A Warrior must do both or the demon can still live. I have a question, though. If beheading a demon alone doesn't work, why didn't that demon yesterday just pop up and come after you before you had set him on fire?"

"Just like anyone else, a demon suffers severe shock and pain when it is injured. Given time and rudimentary care, that demon would have moved again fairly soon." Ouriel perused the long shelves that held our family's weapon collection. "So, with which of these would you prefer to begin?"

I stood, staring stupidly at the mass array of stored weaponry. "Well, the women in my family have all been legendary with a bow and arrow, so I guess I'll start with that."

"Here you are then." Ouriel handed me a bow and a quiver of arrows. "Where is the practice range?"

"On the other side of the basement. Come on." I led the way slowly. The weapon was clumsy in my hands, and I felt outrageously self-conscious. I was terrified I was about to make a fool of myself.

We reached the practice range and my palms started sweating. I fought the urge to run to the bathroom and vomit out my anxiety.

"You are right-handed, are you not?" The query prevented me from making a break for it.

I swallowed with difficulty. "Yes."

"Good. Now, align yourself with your left shoulder facing the target, keeping both shoulders at a right angle to it, and place your feet shoulder width apart and parallel to one another."

I did what he said and allowed him to show me the proper placement of the bow in my hands. I trembled, but not so much from his touch as from my burning insecurities. When he saw how hopeless I was bound to be with this thing, would he still think I was worth his interest?

"Now you are going load the arrow from above and place it on the arrow rest here. Then you'll pull the string all the way back to your nose and aim straight down the arrow. The fingers holding the string should be at your chin."

My arms were beginning to shake, and I didn't even have an arrow in my hands yet. I was a nervous wreck, but Ouriel plowed right on, not even noticing.

"To release your arrow, you're going to let go, pulling straight back and dropping your elbow. Like this." He guided my arm through the appropriate motion. "Are you ready to try it?"

"No." I started laughing and didn't think I could stop.

Ouriel caught me up in a hug. "It is going to be all right, Rose. You can do this. Trust me to teach you."

Strengthened by his faith in me, I fought to get myself under control. He moved behind me, and I took the stance he had just demonstrated. I loaded the bow with the arrow he handed me and pulled the string, just as he had said, and tried the release.

I missed the target.

Completely.

"Well, your form was perfect, but I think you forgot to aim."

"Yeah, I guess I skipped that part." Thank goodness the walls in the basement were cinderblock.

"I also think you might try keeping your eyes open." He sounded curiously like he was choking on something.

"So help me, Ouriel, if I turn around and you are laughing, I'm going to use this thing on you at point blank range!" I looked behind me and saw Ouriel bent over, busying himself with arranging my arrows. "Are you laughing?" I asked with as much menace as I could summon.

He straightened and gave me a wide-eyed, innocent look. "Me? Laugh?" He doubled over again, shaking silently.

"You're a butt," I managed haughtily.

"I am sorry. I will stop. Really. Here, try again." He handed me another arrow. "If you hit the target this time, I can show you how to retrieve the arrow."

That did it. I was thoroughly ticked off now.

I loaded the bow, pulled back, and, sparing only a cursory moment to aim, let my arrow fly. To my amazement, it didn't just hit the target—it hit dead center.

"Holy crap, Rose! That was good!"

"Give me another arrow." I held out my hand for more ammunition. "And did you just say holy crap?"

CHAPTER 9

I found myself, suddenly it seemed to me, in the lunch line with Ouriel and Taylor nearly a month later on a Friday. Time had run past me in a blur of school and exercise. Ouriel was in a hurry to get me in good shape as soon as possible, so I could "train in earnest." I had no idea what that meant. I also wasn't very eager to find out, seeing as his regimen already had my body whining in constant complaint.

Taylor had made a habit of sitting with Ouriel and me every day at lunch, and Ana had made it her own lunchtime habit to bore holes in the backs of our heads with her hateful green eyes. The Taylor part of the routine I had come to thoroughly enjoy, but I could have done without Ana's contribution. She had made it clear that a showdown between us would someday be necessary.

I laughed to myself at the thought. Still, it seemed apt for the animosity that simmered on her side.

"So, um, would you guys like to…you know…maybe do something this weekend?" Taylor broke into my melancholic thoughts. She was bravely fighting a fit of shyness and the blush that was rising in her face.

I looked at Ouriel. I had no decision making power in that area. It was his choice as to whether or not he wanted to risk my safety by going anywhere. I couldn't invite Taylor over either—at least until my life gained some semblance of normalcy. It was a new dilemma for me. I'd never had a true friend before. How strange that I should find one now, when pursuing any kind of meaningful relationship was nearly impossible.

I snapped back to the conversation when Ouriel said, "You know what, Taylor? I think that would be—er—cool. What do you think, Rose?"

"That sounds great. But what are we going to do? Where would we go?" I tried to keep any anxiety out of my voice. I didn't want Taylor to mistake it for reluctance, but the logistics of the thing concerned me.

"I think we should go to the movies," Ouriel spoke up before Taylor had a chance to respond.

Her strained expression relaxed into one of sheer joy. It had probably taken a lot for her to suggest an outing. I suspected she might be as socially challenged as I was—which was a sad, sad thing.

"Okay!" She smiled. "What are we going to see?"

"We'll figure it out tonight." I looked to Ouriel for confirmation of my statement. "When I get home, I'll look up the listings on the Internet, and I'll call both of you. Then we can decide. Okay?"

"Cool with me." Taylor stood to take her tray to the washing window.

"Me, as well." Ouriel tossed me a confidential smirk. "May I suggest we go tomorrow in the early afternoon?"

"That's fine with me," Taylor replied.

"Um…yeah…me too." I'd almost forgotten I had to pretend to agree.

"It is settled then. Rose, you call us tonight and set up a time for us to meet tomorrow at the theatre." The bell rang, and Ouriel sprang up from his seat.

"Crap! Guys, I don't have your numbers!" Rushing out of the cafeteria and across the blacktop, I reached for the cell phone shoved inside the waistband of my skirt.

"Don't worry. We'll meet at the lockers after school, and I'll give you mine then!" Taylor called back, racing into the school building ahead of me.

☙❧☙

When we jumped into the front hallway of my house that afternoon, Ouriel pulled me into the living room and pushed me onto the couch. "I have a question for you."

"Go for it."

"You have worked diligently this week, and we are going to have plenty of time to continue that over the weekend, so—I thought you might be interested in taking the night off."

"None of those sentences were questions," I interrupted, smiling. "But I'm game for having a night off."

"Those were not meant to be the question. If you would allow me to finish—"

"Sorry," I interjected again.

"Rose, seriously—"

"Did you just say seriously? Seriously?" I giggled. Ouriel's eyebrows drew together in a frown, and I knew I had begun to annoy him. "Okay, I'm sorry. Really. Please finish."

"Well, if you are quite done..." Ouriel waited to see if I would open my mouth again, and, when I didn't, he continued, "I was informed last night that Ishmael's condition has improved. In fact, it has improved so much he was able to return to his earthly place of residence yesterday."

I smothered a squeal.

"So, my question is—would you like to visit him?"

"Seriously, Ouriel? I can see him *tonight*?" I couldn't believe it. I'd been waiting for what felt like an eternity.

"Yes." He laughed. "You seriously may. We must wait for cover of darkness to make the Jumps easier, but he will be expecting us shortly after nightfall."

"Oh, Ouri! Thank you! *Thank you*! I can't wait!" I bounced up and down and tried to hug him and kiss him on the cheek. "Wow! I get to see Ishmael, go to a movie, *and* I don't have to run. All in one weekend!" It couldn't get any better for me.

Ouriel barked out a laugh and hugged me back—probably to keep me from jumping around more. "All right, Rose, you are making me dizzy. Calm down." He laughed again. "So, before I tell you of the other surprise I have for you, what would you like to do until then?"

"Another surprise? Holy crap! I don't know if I can take anymore…uh…okay…I do want to change out of my prison garb here, and, then, I don't know. Maybe we could hang out and talk a little bit? About you?" I hesitated when I saw a scowl creep across Ouriel's face. I rushed on, before he could give me a denial. "If that's okay, I mean. I just want to know more about you and—well—all Warriors in general. I never thought to ask Ishmael a lot of things I'm suddenly curious about."

Ouriel's face relaxed a little. He smiled ruefully at the hopeful look in my eyes. "All right. I will attempt to field your questions. Just consider yourself warned that some I may not be able—or willing—to answer."

"I'll understand. I promise." I turned to leave and thought of one last thing. "Oh, and Ouriel, I like the way your laugh sounds."

Before he could recover his composure enough to answer, I ran to change in my room and left the bathroom to Ouriel. We met up in the living room when we were done.

"So what's your other surprise for me?"

Ouriel smiled as he led me to the door. "We must go to the back porch to see it."

I walked out onto the patio and saw a new, beautiful sapling in the center of the yard, still in its pot.

"Is that it?" I hesitated only for a second before I dashed over to examine it more closely.

"Yes. I know that you have been stewing for weeks in search of a way in which to memorialize Javier. I thought, seeing as he loved gardening, this might be a fitting way to do so. It is an orange tree."

I found it difficult to swallow around the boulder that sprang into my throat. I hadn't been able to control my grief enough to even think about what to do for Javi.

"You see," he went on, "rather than being merely decorative, this tree will bear fruit every year. When you harvest it, you may take a moment to remember the fruit Javier's life and work bore for you."

"It's perfect," I whispered.

Ouriel and I quickly set about the work of planting the living memorial in my yard. After we had finished and admired our work, Ouriel threw himself down into a lawn chair. His eyes had gone flat and a muscle ticked in his jaw. I didn't understand his swift change in mood until he spoke.

"I am now prepared for the questions you wished to ask me. What is it you want to know?"

"Ouriel, it's not like I'm about to put you through the Spanish Inquisition, you know."

"I know. And please do not mention that time period to me. I do not have fond memories of it. Many faithful were persecuted, tortured, or put to death for petty jealousies and avarice thinly disguised as piety."

"Okay...so you hate the Spanish Inquisition. That's something I didn't know about you before." I floundered for something I could say without sounding stupid—and failed. It registered vaguely in my mind that the Inquisition had taken place roughly 500 years before, the same amount of time since the death of Ouriel's mother. Was that only a coincidence?

"I despise any and all persecution based on humans' limited understanding of faith." Ouriel jumped back up to prowl around the porch. "You see, what humans do not realize is that every division, every schism, every holy war, was brought about by demons hungry for souls and the destruction of the human race. It is how they seek their revenge on the Creator—discord among His faithful. It is disgustingly simple. Humans are easily divided and happy enough to kill one another over any of the slightest differences in religious practice."

He pinned me with tortured eyes. "I have spent the greater part of 400 human years rectifying the carnage that demons have wrought upon humanity. It is crushing to fight against those humans willing to commit atrocities all in the name of the one God—a being who would never, could never, condone them."

"And that is why Warriors never practice one specific religion," I murmured.

"Correct. All legitimate monotheistic worship springs from the same God. Some forms are truer to Him than others, but, if they are honestly concerned with faith, most of today's major religions will lead people closer to God. Warrior practices encompass the true aspects of each of them."

"Yeah, but it's so easy for you. You *know* the truth. You've been in the presence of God. It's much more difficult for us humans. We have to try to figure out what's true all on our own." I couldn't figure out how to word what I wanted to say. "And I can't even complain. At least as one of Guardian family, I *know* there is a God. The Sightless have to take it all as a matter of faith. Can't you see how difficult that must be?"

"I do see it, and I feel for them. By the same token, I greatly admire all humans of faith and know they will be rewarded. Why do you think God chose to place them first? Why do you think He loves you best of His creations? Because humans alone could be capable of an act as great as believing without having Seen."

His response caught me off guard. I hadn't realized that there could ever be a reason for a Warrior to admire humans. And, human as I was, I had never stopped to wonder just why we were God's favorites. I had just taken it as a given and that, somehow, that was just the way it was supposed to be.

"Wow. I actually get that."

"These are things, as a Guardian, you should know, Rose. You should have learned this long ago. And I had meant to give you a night off, but here you have me exploring some of the deepest, most difficult areas of faith!" Ouriel brushed aside his frustration with my lack of education and smiled at me. "Come, I did not mean to travel this road with you tonight. You must have other questions less theological."

Still lost in the glow of a new understanding, it took me a second to try to remember the things I had meant to ask him earlier. Ouriel had so electrified my brain with his words it took a full minute before I could figure it out.

"Give me a second here. I got sidetracked too." I paused. *Aha*! I remembered one. "Okay, so exactly how old are you, and how does the age thing work for you guys?"

"It is interesting you should ask that tonight." He plopped down in the chair next to me. "Tomorrow is what you could call my birthday."

"Really? Warriors have birthdays? How old are you?"

"Well, it does work a bit differently for us. As you know, we are born with adult understanding, though we are physically immature. We reach that particular milestone at what humans would call puberty. For us, that is around 1200 to 1400 human years old."

"Okay, so how old are you?" I asked, trying not to sound as impatient as I felt.

Ouriel laughed. "Well, a Warrior 'year' is the equivalent of one hundred human years. So, technically, this entire year is like my birthday, although tomorrow does mark the occasion exactly."

Ouriel paused. I was pretty sure he was stalling only to aggravate me.

"So, how old *are* you?" I demanded. I was done pretending to be patient.

"I am 19, in Warrior years, Rose."

"Then you were born in…108 AD?"

"Yes."

"Happy birthday!" I did some quick math in my head. "Wow! So you are 1,883 years older than I am." I giggled. "I think you might be robbing the cradle with me, you know, just a little."

"I do not find that comical." Ouriel grimaced. "If I were a human, I would be less than two years older than you are. I choose to see it that way."

"Yes—we are close in age, *if* you look at it that way. Or you could just be long dead." I laughed again as I leaned over and smacked his arm. I gasped when my hand hit what felt like solid rock. "Ow!"

He grabbed my hand and scoured it for injury. "Are you all right?"

"Yes, I'm fine," I snapped, yanking my hand back. Despite my frustration, a quick glimpse of the scowl on Ouriel's face caused me to burst out laughing. "I guess I should have known better."

"Yes, you should have. Remember that in the future."

"I will. Don't worry." I patted him on the arm that had just nearly broken my hand. "Next time, I'll use my bow and arrow."

He winced. "Please do not jest about that. You have become much too proficient with it in a short amount of time. You might actually cause me permanent damage."

"Whatever, Ouri." I stifled any further laughter because I had just remembered one last question. "Answer one more thing for me before we go look for a movie and call Taylor."

"What is it?" he asked, wary again.

"Well, it actually has to do with the movie. I'm guessing you've noticed that you kind of...well...glow in the dark."

His brow furrowed in confusion. "Yes. All Warriors do."

"I'm also guessing you've noticed that humans don't. So, my question is, how are you going to sit next to Taylor, not to mention all the other Sightless people in the theatre, for two hours? How will they not notice that you look like one of the characters at the end of a *Touched by an Angel* episode?"

"Rose, did you never go out with Ishmael at night?"

"Um...no. I've never really been anywhere out of the house at night." That sounded pathetic even to me. "Everybody's usually working—you know—fighting demons, so I just find ways to entertain myself around here." I spoke that fact as lightly as I could. I didn't want him to see how lonely my existence really was. Most days, it was like I lived alone. Ishmael was with me throughout the school day, but once I was home, I was pretty much the only person there. Ish usually stayed around for an hour or two in the afternoons, and Miriam and Shad ate dinner with me on their off days. Otherwise, I was on my own and had become a microwave chef extraordinaire and book aficionado at a very young age—not to mention a television and movie connoisseur.

"Oh." Ouriel's tone implied that he'd picked up on all I'd left unsaid. "Well, Warriors can quench the 'glow.' At least for a short time. It is not the easiest task to accomplish, but, once a Warrior has mastered the skill, he or she can keep the incandescence to a minimum for a few hours." He paused. "How else did you think we went on patrols at night?"

"I guess I'd never thought about it before." I shrugged. "Honestly, I never really paid any attention. Ishmael is the only Warrior I really knew until I met you."

"Ah, Rose, you have led an incredibly sheltered life. I wonder just how much of that was your own choosing…yet, you've rarely complained, have you?"

I had no idea how to reply to that, so I dashed off to my room. Ouriel followed and sat next to me on the bed as I cracked open my laptop. It took me only a few minutes to find the perfect movie for our Saturday afternoon outing. Many of the weekend's new offerings were too dark for me. My mood wasn't going to allow for anything other than a lighthearted comedy—preferably something romantic.

Ouriel sat next to me as I dialed Taylor's number. When she answered the phone on the first ring, I wondered if she'd been waiting for a call she thought wouldn't come.

"Taylor?" I asked into the receiver.

"Yes, Rose, it's me. Did you find a movie for tomorrow?"

"Yeah. Is it okay if we watch something fun? I don't know about you, but I'm not in the mood for some of the depressing stuff they're showing right now."

"That's cool with me. Which movie do you want to see?" Her end of the line rustled like she was switching her phone from ear to ear.

"Well, there's this romantic comedy coming out that has the sexy dead guy from my favorite hospital show on TV and that guy who played Mr. Darcy in two different movies."

"Oh yeah," she drawled. "I've heard of that one. It's supposed to be pretty cool. The sexy dead guy plays a fireman, right?"

"Yeah, that's the one."

Taylor giggled. "That seals it. I *adore* firemen."

"Okay, I'll meet you for the 12:30 showing at the Carmike? Is that all right? And I'll let Ouriel know too." I had to cover the mouthpiece of my phone so Taylor couldn't hear his snort.

"Um…can I ask you a question first?" Taylor sounded nervous.

"Sure. What is it?"

"Is there something going on between you and Ouriel?"

"What do you mean?" Did she suspect anything? Was it possible she saw past Ouriel's subterfuge? Did she know he wasn't what he seemed?

"Well, I don't mean to be nosy or anything, but have you noticed the way he looks at you?" She paused before rushing on. "I mean, the guy never takes his eyes off of you, and…well…it's like he eats you up with his eyes when you're not looking. He's never more than a few feet away from you and follows you everywhere. Like you're a flame and he's a moth or something."

"Really?" I looked over at Ouriel, who had become very still. I knew he could hear every word she said.

"Yeah. I think he has it pretty bad for you."

"You do?" I tried to keep my voice noncommittal, and Ouriel was quickly turning a color very close to orange. "Maybe someday I'll have the courage to ask him about it."

"If you ask me, you won't have to wait long. I don't see how he'll be able to hold it in much longer." Taylor laughed. "It's great watching Ana nearly combust with jealousy every time she looks at the two of you. By the way, how do you feel about him? You had to have noticed how sexy he is."

It was my turn to blush. Ouriel perked up rather hastily, however. I wanted to smack him for it.

"I…um…well, I'd have to be dead not to notice…" I trailed off, hoping she'd let the subject go.

"Come on, girl. You've got to give me more than that!"

"Well, I guess that I *could* kind of like him, too."

Ouriel quirked an eyebrow at my response.

"Kind of? Are you crazy? I would love to have a guy like that look twice at me!"

"Okay, okay, I might more than 'kind of' like him. And he is pretty sexy. I guess."

"You *guess*? You are so full of it. Admit it! He's freaking hot."

"All right! All right. He's totally gorgeous and just being around him makes me completely out-of-my-mind nervous. Okay?"

"Awesome! I can't wait to start playing matchmaker—"

"Wait!" I cut her off. Ouriel had jumped up and was pacing the floor with a funny expression on his face. "We don't even know if he's interested in a relationship or anything. Let's just wait and see. Okay?"

Taylor blew out an aggravated breath. "If you're sure...I'll wait, but I have to tell you that when a guy looks at a girl like that—well—it—it's usually serious."

"Whatever you say, Taylor. I'm sorry, but I've got to go now. My sister's calling me for dinner. I'll see you tomorrow, though."

"Okay, Rose. Bye!"

I couldn't hang up the phone fast enough. Ouriel and I sat in awkward silence for all of one second before he blurted out, "Well, that was uncomfortable."

"Yeah, extremely." I let loose a sigh of relief, glad he'd spoken first.

"Well, we had best go eat." He headed for the door and stopped, only to smirk at me over his shoulder. "Because, you know that lying, especially to a friend, is a sin. And I would hate to see you *completely* shatter one of the Ten Commandments."

"Shut up!" I stuck my tongue out at his back before getting up to follow him.

"I felt that," he called out.

I could barely restrain the urge to do it again.

When I got to the kitchen, Ouriel was already busy making us both a sandwich. My ire melted at the sight of him moving around, whipping me up something to eat. Could the guy get any sexier? I groaned, went to the cabinet to get some glasses for water, and then set the table.

Of course, because he could work so fast, Ouriel and I made it there simultaneously.

CHAPTER 10

By the time Ouriel and I had finished eating, I was jumping out of my skin to see Ishmael. We cleaned up after ourselves and moved silently toward one another afraid, as always, to even touch. Just as he gathered me into his arms to Jump, Ouriel paused.

"Rose, I want to warn you, before you see Ishmael, that he, well—" Ouriel broke off, floundering for what to say next.

"Spit it out, Ouri!" Anxiety crashed into me so suddenly the euphoria I'd been floating on all evening deflated in one violent implosion. "Seriously, just tell me whatever it is before I have a nervous breakdown!"

"Very well. It seems that Ishmael has not fully recovered from all of the injuries he sustained in the ambush—" Ouriel stopped short to whisper, "Nor will he in future."

"*What*?" My stomach felt like it had sucked itself inside out. "What do you mean?"

"If you will allow me, I *am* trying to explain. Ishmael is still mentally intact—but physically—he will never recover his full faculties."

"So, what you're saying is that he's still Ish, but I shouldn't be too shocked to see that he's permanently disabled in some way?"

"Essentially, yes."

"Well, why didn't you just say that in the first place instead of scaring me half to death?"

Wary in the face of my emotional volatility, Ouriel refrained from pointing out that my constant interruptions were what had extended my own suspense. Instead, he asked, "Well, then, are you ready?" I nodded. "Good. We will be making two Jumps, one each to cover altitude and distance from here. Then we must walk a final short distance, as we cannot merely reintegrate inside a celestial creature's earthly abode."

"Yeah, yeah, I know—special blessings and all that stuff." I was anxious to get there. "Let's go, already!"

Ouriel grinned at me, and we disintegrated, only to reappear in the wilderness of the foothills of the Franklin Mountains. "One more." Ouriel puffed, out of breath. "Are you ready?"

I nodded and took another deep breath. This time, we landed high up on the eastern side of the mountain. I only knew where we were because I could see El Paso's lighted star shining into the darkness of the night just to the south of us. I took a deep breath and shivered only once in the much cooler mountain air.

"I should have planned for more appropriate dress, Rose. I apologize, as we must walk the remaining distance from here." Ouriel rubbed temporary warmth into my bare arms with his hands. "But we are nearly there."

True to his word, Ouriel's glow was nonexistent as we trudged higher up the slope. I couldn't make out a trail, much less a destination, but he led the way without a hint of hesitation. Trusting his unerring, otherworldly eyes, I sent up a prayer of thanks. Left to my own devices, I'd have been tumbling down the mountainside in a cloud of dust.

As we walked just a bit farther, an ephemeral glow began to emerge just ahead of us, appearing slowly as if an invisible fog was lifting. I made out the shape of a small shack with two windows and one door shimmering ahead. It seemed rundown. A building—if anyone ran across it hiking—that was a remnant of a long ago time when El Paso was merely a stop along the *Camino Real* and the land surrounding it was a vast wilderness.

"Is *that* it?" I gasped, barely able to restrain myself from sprinting for the door just ahead.

"Yes." Ouriel smiled and, reading my mind, tugged me into a jog for the cabin. When we arrived at the doorstep, he gestured toward the building. "All you have to do is knock."

I did as Ouriel told me with my heart in my throat. The door swung open to reveal Ish sitting, reclined, in front of a crackling fire, and a Warrior, most likely a

Healer, hovering just beyond him in what passed for the kitchen in Ish's one room shack. I hardly registered the presence of a bed tucked into a corner and a small kitchen table. Ishmael claimed all of my attention. Wordlessly, he held his arms out, and I ran for him, sobs bursting from my throat. I slowed only long enough to arrange myself gently in his lap.

The moment his arms wrapped around me, the second his scent filled my nostrils, a release of anxiety so great shivered through me that it only left tremors in its wake. My response to finally seeing Ishmael in the flesh was so visceral, so instinctual, I was rendered once again a traumatized four year old clinging to the only parent she had left in the world.

"I have missed you so much, Ish!" I whispered into his neck as tears of agony burned their way down my face and into the creases of his warm, amber skin.

Ishmael drew back and seemed to devour all he could of my presence in one gulp. "As I have missed you, my darling girl."

After the initial excitement began to wear off, I noticed I was sitting somewhat off kilter on his lap. I looked down. It took a full minute for my brain to process what I saw.

Part—*most*—of Ishmael's left leg was missing.

"Ish! Your leg! What happened?" I slapped my hand over my lips. I didn't know whether to cry from embarrassment or the realization that Ish had lost his leg for me.

Ishmael only chuckled. "Ah, my darling, I have missed that mouth of yours almost as much as the rest of you."

His retort surprised a giggle out of me. "I'm sorry Ish. I just...I—" I broke off, unable to express the pain or guilt I felt for what had happened.

"Are you, by chance, feeling responsible for my present condition?"

"No," I lied, forgetting for the moment how aware he was of my moods.

"Yes, you are." He chucked me under the chin. "Do not tell me fibs, young lady. You know better."

"I'm sorry. I've just missed you so, so much. I can't even believe I'm getting to see you now." I broke into fresh sobs. As much as I'd craved his presence for an entire month, it hurt to look at Ishmael. I couldn't help noticing the peachy pale color of his skin and the new lines of fatigue scoring his beloved face. My heart broke all over again.

"I love you, Ish." The words seemed ripped from the deepest parts of me. "Thank you for saving me. Again." As a child, he'd kept my spirit from dying along with my parents, and, now, he'd saved me from a fate possibly worse than death.

"Ah, Rose, I would give so much more than one measly leg for the safety of a girl the likes of you."

"Don't say that!" I choked, trying to smack his arm and squeegee the streaming snot from my face all at the same time. Without any real desire to do either, I dropped my head onto his shoulder and shot the most dazzling grin I could muster at him. I also sent up a silent prayer of gratitude. My heart felt full enough to explode from the sheer joy of being with my two favorite Warriors. The love I could feel pulsing through the room was almost palpable.

A soft movement behind me splintered the quiet of my reverie, and I heard the muted tones of the Healer say, "I am sorry, Ishmael, but it is time for your guests to take their leave."

"Already?" I sniffled. "But we just got here."

"I know, dear, but I cannot have him overly drained." She reached to straighten Ishmael's cover when I stood. "And you are perfectly welcome to return tomorrow."

"Would that be okay, Ouri? Can we come back tomorrow?"

Ouriel blinded me with a grin. "I believe I can work it into our itinerary."

If I hadn't already been in love with the guy, I would have fallen then. He knew how necessary Ishmael was to my happiness and my sanity.

"Very well." Ishmael's eyes drooped with exhaustion. "Then it is all settled. I will see you tomorrow, darling child, and you as well, Ouriel my boy. I am grateful to you for assuming responsibility for Rose's care so seamlessly."

Ouriel bowed slightly. "It is I who will always be indebted to you, Ishmael, sir."

"Not true, son, but I will ask you to protect her with your very life, if need be, as I would."

"Do not doubt that I would, sir."

"Good then—"

"Hey, guys, cut it out with all the dying talk. It sucks!" I didn't want to think about losing either of them for a moment. It made my heart feel like it would drop out of my chest—and then out of my body entirely.

"I am sorry, dear." Ishmael's steely gaze didn't leave Ouriel's. When he did turn to me at last, Ishmael said, "Now, I will say goodbye for tonight. I love you. May God speed and bless you both."

"And the Creator's blessing upon you, sir." Ouriel inclined his head.

I was able to squeeze Ishmael in a hug one last time and whisper a hasty, "I love you," before I was half dragged, half pushed out of the building by the Healer and Ouriel. I passed over the threshold and turned for another glimpse of Ish, but he was already nodding off to sleep.

Ouriel reached for my hand and guided me back down the trail to our Jump point in silence.

છળછળ

Late the next day, Ouriel popped into my foyer just as I was heading out of the bathroom and a makeup lesson with Gen. I felt rather proud of myself as Ouriel surveyed the work I had just completed on my face. I was beginning to believe I might actually get the hang of this girly crap someday.

I was also very excited at the prospect of going to the movies with Taylor. I had never had a friend I felt comfortable enough to "hang out" with. All the kids my age I'd known before going to Sightless school were from Guardian families and, thanks to my differences, I'd never really become close to any of them. In fact, most were already out fighting, whether they did so with their families or the clans who lived near where they'd decided to go to college. Needless to say, the kids at school had never really been to my liking either, so I was ecstatic to have finally found someone like Taylor who might become a true friend.

Of course, the idea of going to the movies with Ouriel as my sort-of-kind-of-but-not-really boyfriend was pretty cool too.

Who was I kidding?

I was shaking with nerves of titillated anticipation.

"Rose?" Ouriel's voice broke into my daydream.

"Uh…yeah?" I floated back to reality.

"Are you ready to go? I have arranged to drive your grandfather's truck. It shouldn't take us long. We have only a few miles to travel, once we come to the expressway. Luckily, we do not even need to concern ourselves much with stoplights along the way."

"Great." I really hated that vehicle. "I am *so* glad we're driving."

"Is that sarcasm, Rose? Why would the drive bother you?" Ouriel didn't get my reluctance to ride around in what most guys probably thought was a cool classic truck.

"No reason. I just hate riding in that rumbly old thing. It likes to shake the fillings out of my teeth."

"Well…" Ouriel looked a bit confused. "It will not be a long drive, so I hope it will not inconvenience you too terribly."

I laughed at Ouriel's inability to grasp the pettiness of my grumblings. "It's okay. I'll be fine. I just like to complain about it. I have ever since my parents used to drive me around in it."

"Well, shall we go then?"

He offered me his arm like an English gentleman out of a Jane Austen novel. Giggling even more now, I accepted the proffered limb and allowed him to guide me out to the carport on the side of our house. In my great-grandparents' time, it had been more of a carriage house. And, just as my grandfather would have, Ouriel handed me up into the cab of the truck. He circled around quickly to the driver's side while I buckled myself in.

My emotions ran amok. I was flying high on the joy of going on my first date and waxing nostalgic over how many generations of men in my family had taken their women out on the town from this spot. Even the cracked dashboard and steering wheel of the truck brought to mind all of the people, most now dead, who had driven me around in this truck. How could something so wonderful mix with the terrible so easily? And what was wrong with me, misting up about the past when I should, for once, be thinking hopefully of the future?

A shudder ran though me once again as Ouriel turned the key and the ignition blasted the truck into life. Desperately, I hugged myself back into the present and tried to spread some heat back into my body.

"Are you all right?" Ouriel asked abruptly, sending me clawing for the ceiling of the cab.

"Uh…yeah. I'm just excited. I've never done anything like this with friends. I think my adrenaline just kicked into super spaz mode. Sorry!" I laughed a hollow sound, trying to throw Ouriel off the scent of my unease. I forced myself into a brighter mood. I was not going to let the bloody deaths of my family take this first moment of freedom from me. It was too precious. I was finally doing something apart from family, Guardian life, and demons.

I would *not* ruin it.

With a real smile, I leaned closer to the window so the air could blow my hair away from my face. I didn't even let the lack of air conditioning causing my hair to muss and tangle bother me. Ouriel turned, at the stop sign just down from my house, and shot me one of those rare smiles of his, and I knew he was feeling the same way I did. All the ugliness we'd seen, all the loss of life—none of that was going to mess with our heads today. This time was for us. A stolen moment of pleasure.

Too soon, we pulled into the parking lot and walked up to find a nervous Taylor pacing in front of the box office.

"Hi guys!" she chirped, walking toward us. "I've already got our tickets. I figured you could buy the popcorn and soda. Is that okay?"

"Actually, that sounds great. You ladies should go find us seats while I get the refreshments," Ouriel replied. "What would you like?"

"I want some popcorn and a Pibb Xtra," I said, raising my hand like a second grade dork.

"Um…I think I want water and M&M's." Taylor dug in her pocket. "Oh, and here's your ticket. We'll see you inside!"

Ouriel went his way as Taylor and I wound through the hallways to our specific theatre. We picked the best spot we could that had an aisle seat for Ouriel. I figured he'd need the extra space to stretch out his obnoxiously long legs.

By the time the Warrior joined us, the previews were playing across the screen. We all settled in with little chitchat to watch a delightfully fluffy piece of romantic nonsense. Sadly, my time in fantasyland passed too quickly, and, before I knew it, the credits were rolling. The movie had been just what I needed to get away from my own life for a while.

"Oh! That was so good!" Taylor squealed. "I just *love* love stories. Don't you?"

Ouriel gave no answer, but I nodded in agreement with her. "I do. It's nice to see people happy."

"Isn't it?" she asked. "There's enough ugly and sad in the real world. I don't want to see it during my fun time. I see plenty in real life, you know?"

I sensed something deeper in Taylor than the light-hearted persona she always presented at school and couldn't help but wonder what her pain was. It dawned on me that we all had our own demons, even people as mild as Taylor always seemed to be.

"Right?" I finally blurted out.

"I usually prefer something a bit more masculine," Ouriel intoned, and Taylor and I were forced to stifle giggles. "But this movie did seem to lighten my mood somewhat."

My friend and I let his comment go with only a smiling look to one another. Someday, maybe soon, Ouriel was going to learn to take life less seriously. He *had* to learn—if only to keep me from dying of a giggle overdose.

We walked out into the bright El Paso sunshine, each of us flinching. The glare was almost painful after the darkness of the theatre. I found my mood sinking a bit as I realized my outing was about to be over, and I tried not to let it show. We had to wait a few minutes for Taylor's parents to pick her up—she had texted them just before the movie ended.

Before she could leave, I pulled her into a quick hug. "We need to do this again. Really. And soon."

"Definitely!" she beamed back at me and climbed into the car.

"Are you ready to go see Ishmael?" Ouriel asked me, as we watched her drive away.

"Yep," I sighed. "Come on, let's take the truck back to the house and get going." My real life was waiting for me. My own personal demons were all too ready to remind me of their stabbing presence in the tenderest parts of my heart—where my love and guilt for Ishmael lived.

We landed high up on the mountain, somewhere near the place we had the night before. Again, I couldn't see Ishmael's house from where we were, but Ouriel turned immediately to the trail and began walking uphill. Miriam trailed close behind him. She'd wanted to see Ishmael too, and Ouri'd been happy to have another seasoned guard dog along. *Maybe they're right to be so worried, but I don't get it.* I shook my head. The thought that I was wanted by demons just didn't compute.

I dragged along behind them, trying not to think too much about the ghosts who had returned to haunt me earlier. My heart felt heavy with the grime of all the suffering my family, Ouriel, and I had seen. I could feel the weight all the way down to the soles of my feet, and I slugged even more despondently toward my stand-in father and the wreck I had made of his body.

I was so engrossed in feeling sorry for myself that I barely even felt the mosquito I reached up to slap absentmindedly off the back of my neck. Lost to all but my own pity party, it didn't register in my mind that all the mosquitoes in El Paso were usually dead by the end of September.

I didn't notice the demons until one had his arm clamped around my throat.

Choking, I looked around and saw we were surrounded.

I didn't have to think before I reached for the knife at my back. Instinct and training took over, and I slammed

my gift from Ouriel into the abdomen of the demon holding me. He dropped to the ground. I turned to stab him a
few more times, to keep him out of the fight a bit longer,
and then ran for Miriam and Ouriel. He had picked up his
sword when we dropped off the truck and was already
busy slicing the heads off at least five demons. My sister
was rapidly firing off arrow after arrow, sinking as many
as left her quiver into demon flesh. But more kept popping in all around us.

I can't say how many demons I cut and sliced with
my knife and nails to get to my sister and my Warrior,
but I got through enough to guard their backs. Finally, the
three of us stood back to back, facing down the enemy.
Ouriel slipped me his knife, and both of my hands became deadly. We slashed wildly, and I cursed myself for
not strapping on my bow and arrows for the trip. Behind
me and out of breath, Ouriel shouted, "Miriam, get Rose
out of here! Run for Ishmael's house. I will cover you!"

"No way!" I yelled back. "I'm *not* leaving you!"

Ouriel decapitated two more of the demons rushing
him. "You have to!"

"*No!*" I screamed and took down one of my own,
kicking and jabbing her into a bloody pulp.

"We can't hold them all off," Miriam panted. "And I
must save you at all costs."

Ouriel spun and, in one fluid move, gored a demon
and pushed me through the opening toward Ishmael's
house.

Shocked, I stumbled right into the arms of the older
Warrior himself. I looked down stupidly, wondering how

Ishmael could stand with only one leg. I saw only a bright golden mist shining where the limb should have been.

"Ish? How? What—" I didn't even have time to get out a complete thought.

"Get back!" He shoved me roughly behind him. With one last, loving look, Ish called out, "This I give to you, my daughters," and waded into the fray as though he had two working legs.

I couldn't seem to move when I saw Ishmael grab Ouri and throw him toward me. "Get her out. Now!"

With a nod, Ouriel scooped me up and Jumped away. As soon as my mind caught up with my body, I flailed against the iron hold of his arms. I kicked and screamed and bit at him, trying to keep him from Jumping me any farther than the foothills of the mountain.

"Go back! Go back now!" I shrieked. *Dear God, where's Miriam?* I couldn't see if she'd Jumped with us or not. Maybe I could get away before Ouriel regrouped enough to Jump me home. "Leave me!" I begged. "Save them! Please."

A countenance of stone was Ouriel's only response. He restrained me mercilessly for the next Jump. I looked uphill toward where I knew Ish was sacrificing himself for me and saw, just barely, a fighting figure with mist for a leg being Jumped away by two demons.

e⁊e⁊

"*How could you?*" were the only words I could manage as we appeared in my kitchen. "Go back! Now!" I pummeled Ouriel's chest with my fists over and over again.

He grabbed for wrists, pulled me hard against his body, and twisted my arms behind my back. "I am!"

Unable to hear his words through blinding agony, I tried to bite his neck.

Ouriel shook me. "Rose, listen to me! I. Am. Going. Back."

His words penetrated my rage, and I stilled. "Then go already!" Spurred on by adrenaline and fear, I grabbed Ouriel by the back of his neck, latched my body onto his, and scorched him with a kiss. It took him a second to respond, but when he did, I was rocked to the core. He crushed his mouth onto mine and anchored my body to his. Only the thought of Ishmael could force me to let him go. I pulled away.

"Be careful—please," I whispered into his neck.

"I love you, Rose." Ouriel rested his now-chaste lips on my forehead. "I will find him for you or die trying. You must go quickly to find your sisters and prepare yourselves for what it may take to save him. I will return in less than an hour."

The stupid Warrior didn't even let me say I loved him too or ask him to please not die before he was gone.

Nearing overload, I allowed myself only one second to descend into the madness of tears before I ran screaming for Miriam, clueless as to if—or where—she'd landed from her emergency Jump.

CHAPTER 11

I felt like my body was digesting itself slowly from the inside out. I had never felt fear, more like abject terror, as I did in the seemingly interminable hours I waited for Ouriel to come back from chasing Ishmael. I looked absently around, barely taking in the worried looks on the faces of my sisters and brother-in-law. *At least Miri made it home.*

But where was Ouriel?

It had been two hours—one hour too long—since he had promised to return with news of Ishmael. I was starting to fear the worst. I didn't know how I would be able to deal with any of it if Ishmael was dead.

How could I go on without him?

The Warrior who had served as my father for the last thirteen years was more than just a parental figure to me. He was my best friend, the one being I ran to with every minute detail of my boring existence. Whether I came to him with my joys or sorrows, Ish had been there for me throughout the entirety of my sentient life.

Who would I run to if he were no longer here?

Ishmael was, had always been, my anchor. Without him, I was pretty sure I would be lost in a sea of despair so great even Ouriel might not be able to find me and fish me out.

Worse still, what if Ouriel never came back either? I'd been the one screaming at him to go after Ishmael. Not that I'd had a choice, but what if I lost them both?

I put my hand to my mouth to stifle the sob that exploded from my chest. I stopped pacing and grabbed for the back of a kitchen chair. My shoulders shook with the racking weight of my mental anguish, and I found myself repeating, "Please, God, give me the strength. I don't think I can do this much longer!" trying to ward off any more pain.

Hearing my whispered pleas, Miriam rose from her place at the table to put a soft hand on my shoulder.

"Rose, honey—" she began, but her words were interrupted by the sound of a slamming door.

Briathos burst into the kitchen with such force and urgency my heart very literally stopped.

Shadrach jumped to his feet. "Do you have news?"

Briathos's eyes flicked to me, and his face crumpled with the effort of forming his next words. "My intelligence agents just reported back. The demon horde does indeed hold my brother hostage. And, it seems, my son as well."

It felt like my mind had been cast into a pit of quick sand. I couldn't seem to form any kind of coherent thought. I struggled to find meaning in the few sentences Briathos had uttered. I couldn't force myself to think, but I still felt entirely too much. *Why can't I shut it all off? It's too much!*

My entire world had just imploded.

The room and my head began to spin, and I ran for the bathroom. For a crazy moment I could see the inane hilarity in the fact that I always reacted to bad news by fainting or puking. Any idiotic notions of humor were forgotten, though, as I heaved violently into the toilet. At least the physical pain of vomiting kept my suffocating emotional pain at bay for a moment.

I regained physical control soon, however, and my mind began functioning again all too well. Had Briathos just called Ishmael his brother? What on earth did that mean? Had he been speaking figuratively or literally? I immediately knew the answers to those questions, though I didn't like them. Why hadn't Ouriel told me that Ish was his uncle? For that matter, why hadn't Ishmael ever told me that he had living family?

Odd, how a tiny bit of anger for the two people I loved most was able to spark to life within me just then, while they were in such grave danger. The idea caused more frantic laughter to bubble up within me before I could get a hold of myself.

What is wrong with me? Why did these strange thoughts keep worming themselves into my head when I had immensely more important things to worry about?

I looked up from the bathroom sink to stare at my pale reflection in the mirror. I needed to control my feelings, or I'd never be able to help Ouriel or Ish.

Because, without a doubt, Sightless or not, I *was* going to fight for them.

Miriam and Gen had to allow it, even though I wasn't of age. They couldn't keep me trapped at home when all of my family was going to be in danger. That would be torture of the grossest kind.

I gathered my thoughts together and walked out of the bathroom. It felt like my body was no longer my own as I floated down the hall into the kitchen. Sound came to me hazily, as if I was dreaming, but I focused on my family and what was left of Ouri's. They all sat at the kitchen table, methodically trying to work out a battle strategy. *How are they staying so calm*?

Through my agony, I heard only flashes of the conversation.

"…I don't know. My spirits are searching…How many do you think we'll be facing?" That was Gen, ever the pragmatist.

"…had a vision…need to call in those of our legion that can be reached at a moment's notice…" Miriam's voice put in.

"…already trying to help run down my connection to Ishmael through his last message." Shad sounded like he was talking underwater.

"We are going to be severely outnumbered. I do not know how we will manage." The anguish in Briathos's voice, so like Ouriel's, crashed into my body like an ice-cold shower.

"I'm coming too. Count me in."

All the adults in the room broke off and turned to look at me as one. I couldn't begin to name all the emotions that flashed across their faces before the shouting started.

Miriam screamed, "No!"

Shad surged to his feet. "Absolutely not!"

"You don't know what you're saying!" That was from Gen.

Only Briathos remained silent. He seemed to be measuring my determination before he dared utter a word. I couldn't tell what was going on in that Warrior mind of his, but what looked like hope dawned on his face.

When my family had finally shut up, Briathos stood. "As for me, I believe the girl should go with us. We are already terribly undermanned. She may be able to help."

His statement shocked all of us into silence. Each of us gaped at him.

Of all people, he *is going to support my bid to fight?*

It was unreal.

"I absolutely forbid it!" Miriam ground out when she had regained control of herself. "I couldn't focus with her there."

Gen only looked at me, speculative, before she murmured, "Miriam, she might really be able to help. Ouri has been teaching her, and he said she's awesome with a bow and arrow."

Nearly outvoted, Miriam turned to Shadrach, pleading, "She can't go—"

Shad pulled his wife into his arms and turned to me. "Are you sure, Rose? You understand the danger? And that some of us might not come back?"

"Yes." I knew well that I would probably be one of those who didn't make it.

"You will do as you're ordered? Do what is best for all involved, not just whoever it is that you love most?"

"I swear it."

We all looked at Miriam. Everyone knew the final decision lay with her. Not only was she my legal guardian, but she was also commander of all Guardian forces in the city.

"Please, Miri!" I *needed* to serve, at least in some way. "I'll only follow after you're gone anyway."

"Fine." Her voice broke on the word. "But you will stay beside Gen or me the entire time. You will be in my line of sight or hers. Do you understand?"

"Yes, Miriam." I peeled her off her husband and into a hug of my own. "Okay, so now that that's settled, tell me what's going on."

Shad grimaced and dragged a hand through his short hair. "Our first objective right now is to find where Ish and Ouriel are. They both managed to fire off one last message to me before being taken. We tried to trace the waning connection I had with them but only succeeded in pinpointing a general area before the link was severed. We've got it narrowed down to somewhere in the desert near Santa Teresa." Shad pointed at a spot in New Mexico on the map resting on the kitchen table.

"The link was severed? As in you can't feel either of them anymore?" I tried not to think about what that could indicate, and the shifty look on Shad's face wasn't helping. "Does that mean they're—"

"It doesn't mean anything, Rose," Briathos cut in.

"Right," Miriam added. "The one thing I can say for sure right now is that the area we tracked them to matches up with the flashes of Vision I had when I tried to meditate a few minutes ago."

"And now we're just waiting on some of my special friends to report back." Gen sighed. "Then we'll know for sure where we're headed."

It seemed no one wanted to say anything else, and the weight of the silence grated on my nerves.

"Do you guys think we'll actually be able to get them both back? Alive?" I blurted out while trying to contain a shiver. I didn't want to imagine life without either Warrior.

"I don't know." Gen turned toward the window in an attempt to hide the tear trailing down her cheek. "But it's our only chance. We just have to hope that it is God's will that we bring them both home."

"All right, then. We've wasted enough time. Let's get to planning." I nodded and tried to swallow around the lump that had sprung up in the back of my throat. "And, Miriam? Thanks for letting me help. You won't regret it. I promise. I will make you proud."

She smiled at me through the worry in her eyes. "You always have, baby. You always have." With that, she turned and began barking out orders at Shad and Gen, both of whom had already begun scrambling to prepare for the coming battle.

Briathos took his leave and was gone to bring together what Warrior forces he could.

c∽∕e∽∕∂

We all met at an abandoned cotton gin in the desert somewhere near the place that the New Mexico, Texas, and Mexico borders all came together. From our reconnaissance point behind some sand dunes just a short distance away, I could see numerous ramshackle and broken down buildings around what looked like it had once been a thriving cotton farm.

To the west of us, the sun was just setting over the *mesas*, shooting off purple, orange, and red in a last blast of color before nightfall. In the east, the Franklin Mountains burned the same colors, reflecting the brilliance of the desert sunset.

I searched out the familiar outline of Mt. Cristo Rey just to our southeast and noticed that, from my angle, all I could see was the back of the huge statue on its peak. I tried to muster enough courage to mumble a quick prayer, but I couldn't. It was very difficult to talk to someone when it seemed His back was turned—even if it was only a limestone representation of that back.

I dragged my eyes from the landmark and tried to focus on what Miriam was saying to all the Guardians as they continued to Jump in from wherever else their duties had taken them. Briathos was doing the same with the band of Warriors he'd summoned. I kept myself separate from all of them and tried to swallow a panic attack that threatened to overwhelm me.

Gen broke away from Miriam to walk toward me and place a hand on my shoulder. "You can do this, Rose. I know you're scared. And you can probably only think about what awful things we might find in there. But you have to focus that fear. Out of control, it debilitates you. Under control, it strengthens you. Okay?"

Her brow, furrowed with worry, reflected mine. I could only nod my head that I understood.

Separated from it by only a few yards, I hated the look of the cotton gin facing us. What should have been a symbol of past agricultural pride had been twisted into something dark and tormenting in its desolation. More than simply looking like a haven for evil, it exuded some kind of horrible tension in the space around it. It wasn't a feeling I could put into words very well. I just knew great evil roiled under the façade of the seemingly run down group of buildings.

To calm my nerves, I checked my bow and supply of arrows. I felt for Ouriel's knife at my back, and the weight of it steadied me. I knew now, without any doubt, that I could use both to kill in order save the people I loved.

Time before the start of the invasion dwindled, as did the fear of my own death. Losing a loved one tonight would be far more devastating than anything else a demon could do to me. Any thoughts of my own mortality paled in comparison to theirs.

I heard Miriam moving from person to person, giving each one last minute instructions or inspiration. I tried to focus, to hold onto my anger and fear and let them fuel me. I would not give in to either. My focus dissolved only for a moment when Briathos came to stand next to me.

"Thank you. For being here." Briathos's usual veneer, so aloof and similar to his son's that I wanted to reach out to him, broke apart. I could finally see the anguish and love he kept shoved beneath its surface. "I know that I may seem cruel to you at times, but I am not. Centuries of battle have hardened me, but I still love deeply. As does my son. And, apparently, as do you. Although Ishmael and Ouriel will both have my hide for allowing you to be here, your presence and willingness to fight heartens me and gives me hope."

Ouriel's father shocked me with a rare smile—it mesmerized me as totally as the single tear that snaked its way down his amber cheek. When Miriam and Gen walked over to stand with us, I took a deep breath and tried not to panic.

The time for my first offensive had arrived.

Gen grabbed my right hand and squeezed it for reassurance, and I felt Miriam place her hand on my shoulder from behind.

Briathos raised his face skyward and, as one, the crowd around us bowed their heads as he prayed, "Lord, God of heaven and earth, behold their arrogance. Regard our lowliness and look with favor on Your holy ones. Show that You do not abandon those who trust in You, but that You humble those who trust in themselves and glory in their own strength."

Every Guardian and Warrior present amassed behind us, and Briathos shouted, "May God protect us all!"

His powerful voice awakened the fiends within the compound. The sky bled black with rapidly appearing demons. They Jumped in all around us. I drew an arrow, nocked it, and let it fly at the demon nearest me. It struck its target dead in the eye—literally, for the most part. I felt Miriam and Gen turn, both to fight and protect my flanks, as they did the same with their bows.

The first wave of demons fell back under the ferocity of our attack, but I saw that a good number of Guardians began to dot the ground already littered with demon bodies. Briathos bellowed, "Let's go!" from somewhere behind me. A large contingent of Warriors broke off from the main body and followed him in the direction of the building to our left. Miriam, Gen, Shad, and I moved for the building connected to it by a catwalk on the right. A few Warriors remained behind to set fire to the large numbers of disabled demon bodies.

As we ran for the cover of the building, I felt an arrow slice the air to my right and heard the sickening thud of it embedding in human flesh. Next to me, Gen crumpled as the force of the strike took her down. I dove for her and felt for the arrow that now protruded from her left shoulder. I covered her with my own body to protect her from the arrows that continued to rip through the air above us.

"Get her up! Get her to cover!" Miriam screamed. She and I grabbed Gen from either side and lifted her to a standing position.

I felt my sister muster all her strength as she forced her feet to propel her toward the door of the building. Miriam and I half carried her while Shad rushed ahead and broke down the door. Two fledgling demons rushed out at us, and Shad severed their heads from their bodies with his sword.

"Get in here!" Shad turned to cover our retreat. "We don't have much time before they're up again!"

Another slew of arrows rained over us as my sisters and I stumbled through the door.

"We've got only a few moments." Miriam had to yell to be heard over the din of battle. "Gen, do you think you can still Jump out of here?"

"I don't know," Gen slurred. "I'm losing blood pretty fast."

"You can do this, Gen. Our medical post is only two miles from here. You can make a Jump like that in your sleep!" Miriam gathered Gen close enough to Jump her out. "Do you need me to come with you?"

"No! Stay with Rose. I can do it." Gen pushed Miriam aside, tried to sit up, and faltered.

"Gen, let Miriam take you! I'll be fine. Shad is here with me." The blood pooling in large amounts on the floor told me she was running out of time.

"No! One of us has to stay with you, and Miriam's right. I can do this in my sleep. Just sit me up."

I hauled Gen upright. "You can do it," I whispered to her. I held her tight, and Gen grew warm in my arms. "You *can*. And I love you more than I could ever say."

She smiled at me and dissolved.

As soon as she was gone, I snapped back into action and leapt up to follow Miriam and Shad. We secured the rest of the first floor and found a flight of stairs toward the back of the building. We climbed upward with Shad in the lead. Miriam moved to cover my back. We hit the landing and heard a sudden movement on the floor just above us. Stalled, we listened as silently as our ragged breaths would allow and heard what sounded like two sets of footsteps. Something very heavy was being dragged along the tile floor in the hallway outside the stairwell.

When we gained the top landing, my pulse pounded so loudly in my ears that Gen could probably hear it two miles away. Miriam positioned herself opposite Shad at the exit. I nearly froze in admiration of my sister as she kicked down the closed door. Shad burst into the hallway after it, and I followed close behind to cover him.

Two demons were working furiously at a window in the room immediately across the hall from us. They turned and rushed to attack. I caught one with an arrow through the shoulder with such force it pinned him to the wall. Miriam's arrow pierced the second demon a split second before Shad's sword relieved him of his head.

The skewered demon screeched in torment—or excitement, I really couldn't tell which. Miriam slammed the door to the room, shutting us in with the monster.

"Where are they?" she demanded of the demon still attached to his head.

"I don't know what you're talking about," he cackled in his high-pitched, grating voice.

"The Warriors being held captive—where are they?" Shadrach grated out, digging into the demon's neck with the blade of his sword.

The demon shook with another seriously creepy fit of the giggles. "You'll have to guess because I won't tell you!"

Faced with such unabashed evil, my gag reflex kicked in yet again. I quashed it and forced myself to hold eye contact with the demon. As I did so, a strange feeling welled up within me. For the first time in my life, I knew true hatred. The emotion razed through my body, and the inferno of it burned away all the fear, insecurities, and nausea that had plagued me throughout my life. The back of my neck sizzled once again with a prickly sensation.

I could wait no longer for the demon's answer.

"Tell me where they are. *Now!*" I nocked another arrow and aimed for the demon's left eye, which widened in terror.

He broke off his insane laughter and choked. Probably gagging on his own saliva, the demon clawed at his neck and nearly ripped it to shreds in an attempt to breathe. I turned away to forestall feeling any pity for him.

His words hit me like a tsunami from behind. "One of them—well—I—I don't know where he is. The other, though—"

I turned back in time to see him collapse into another fit of cackling.

"The other one what?" I yelled.

Strangling once more, the demon couldn't get anything out past his suddenly too large tongue. His eyes, hysterical now from lack of oxygen, kept darting to the wrapped bundle on the floor near the window. So *that* was what we had heard he and his decapitated counterpart struggling with from the stairwell.

But what was it?

And what had they been doing with it at the window?

Time slowed terribly, and the significance of that bundle hit me.

"Get her out of here!" Shad arrived at the same conclusion just a second before I did. "Get her out! Now!"

My vision clouded. Shad's words confirmed that one of my Warriors was in the room with us. I screamed and dove for the bundle. I didn't reach it before Miriam caught me up by the arm and threw me over her shoulder. She hauled me back into the stairwell. I struggled to gain one last glance at the sack on the floor. All of my senses, except one, seemed to dull. I couldn't see anything, but I could still hear. My ears echoed with demonic laughter. It chased me across the hall and down the stairs, as did Shad's whispered plea, "Dear God in Heaven, may this Warrior's soul find rest in you."

"*No*! Miriam! No! Let me go! Let me go to him!" I thrashed against my sister, but she only clamped me down tighter. "I have to see him. Please."

Couldn't she understand that I had to see who was in that bag?

The absolute knowledge that one of my Warriors was dead dragged the fight out of my body. Miriam sensed it was safe to let me go, and we both fell to the floor on the middle landing.

"Hush, baby, hush," Miriam crooned over and over again.

I barely heard her over the ringing in my ears and a horrible broken wailing that filled the stairwell. When the sound of it reverberated back, I realized the sobs were coming from me. I noticed the shrieking of the demon had long been silenced, and I looked up to find Miriam and Shad's horror-stricken faces staring at me.

"Who?" I gasped, as Shad fell on his knees next to us.

"Ishmael. God help us all, it was Ishmael." Shad's face twisted with grief. "They were—I'm sorry, Rose— they were going to hang his body out the window so we could all see it."

Even though I knew it to be true, I didn't want to believe it. Ishmael couldn't be dead. I'd just seen him this afternoon. And where was Ouriel? I could only think that he might be hanging somewhere right now too. *Dear God, help me*! Disbelief and shock warred with pain.

My heart tore in half.

"No! No, it can't be him. You're wrong, Shad!" I could barely form the words, but I had no trouble jumping to my feet. "I have to see. I have to—"

"No!" Shad lunged in front of me, blocking my view of the hallway and the room behind him. "Trust me, Rose. You don't want that image in your mind. You want to remember Ishmael as you last saw him."

"He's right, baby. You don't want to see Ish this way." Miriam stroked my face then turned to her husband. "Did you secure the body?"

"Yes. He's well hidden."

"*What*? We're just gonna leave him here? You can't! I won't let you." I tried again to run for Ishmael.

"Rose!" Miriam grabbed me by the shoulders and shook me out of my hysteria. Tears streamed down her face. "He was like my father, too, but we have no other choice. We have to find Ouri before it's too late. There's still hope for him."

Miriam was right. I had to gather together the remaining tatters of my sanity.

"He was still alive when that demon in there saw him last." Shad shook his head. "I could See that much from his mind but not much else. He really didn't know anything."

"Okay, so what do we do now?" I wasn't sure I could go on.

"We'll move through the rest of this building to make sure it's secure, and Warriors are following close behind us to ensure that it remains that way. Shad will get a message to them about Ishmael." Miriam wiped any trace of tears from her face and her eyes bored into mine. "Are you ready?"

"Yeah." I sniffed back a gush of tears and mucus that hadn't managed to run onto my face yet. "Let's go."

We left the stairwell once more and moved down the hallway, working to secure each room one by one. I spared only one glance for the place where I'd last seen Ishmael's body. I felt no satisfaction at the sight of the demon's headless carcass still lying there. The end of his existence would never return Ishmael's. At the very least, though, he could never cause another being the pain that continued to tear through my body. The only thing keeping me on my feet was the hope that Ouriel might be somewhere nearby. *Alive*, I thought to myself, willing it to be true. *He will be alive.*

When we reached the end of the hallway, we found a second stairwell that led us out the back of the building. Back on the ground floor, we opened the outside door into a pack of demons. Shad had taken point and stood directly in front of me in the open doorway. Miriam guarded my rear. Before we could react, Shad went down under the weight of two attacking demons. Miriam shoved me roughly to the floor and jumped into the fray, shooting arrows left and right. I focused on Shad from my precarious position and waited for a clear shot at his two demons.

I landed three arrows in each of them.

Unfortunately, that wasn't enough to slow them down, mostly because only their backs had been exposed. I threw down my bow and reached for my Bowie knife. Leaping into the wriggling ball of bodies, I landed on the demon nearest me, grabbed for her head, and made quick work of slitting her throat. I tossed her paralyzed body aside and did the same with the second demon.

Shad had been left almost unrecognizable by the attack. Blood drained from just about every visible place on his body. There were deep gashes in his chest and both thighs. I bent to tend his wounds and heard Miriam scream in pain. My blood soaked hands fumbled for my knife as I bounded up to help my sister.

She was about twenty feet to my left. All else faded from my vision. I saw only Miriam on her knees, a demon claw to her throat. My sister's right arm hung useless by her side.

"No!" Miriam screamed again, when she read the intention in my eyes. "No, Rose! Just run! Get out of here—" Miriam was cut off by a rough yank of her hair.

"Shut up, stupid Guardian," a familiar demoness hissed from behind her. I recognized the female who had tried—and failed—to abduct me twice. "Let the little girl try to save you. I'll enjoy her watching you die."

"Leave her out of this, Melana!"

"Oh my! Is the ever-so-calm-and-calculated Guardian Commander's resolve finally shaken?" Melana grinned hideously. "Tell me, Miriam dear, just what are you willing to do to save your sister?"

Miriam's eyes met mine. My treacherous gag reflex responded instantly to the emotion in them. "Miriam!" I begged. "Miriam, don't!"

"I will not give my soul for her, but I will die for her to live."

"Oh, that's too bad. Your death just won't be enough to ransom her."

"No! Melana, wait!" I choked back my tears and my need to vomit. "I will trade myself for her. Just let her go."

"Well now, how sweet! I have two lovely sisters here offering to die for one another. Too bad *both* of you will have to die. Little one, you will watch this one die for you in vain, and, Miriam, you will know before you die that I will take this girl to my master after you are gone!"

Rage blazed within me. "You will not kill my sister, demon!"

"And who's going to stop me?"

"I will."

"Ha! You're not even a Guardian. I've heard tell you can't even See. What do you have that is more powerful than I am?"

"I have love, and I have God."

"God didn't save your parents from my master. Why would He save you?"

Melana's question hit me with the accuracy of a Kazin woman's arrow, but doubt didn't overcome me as it would have in the past. I felt the answer welling inside me and bursting out of my mouth before I could even process the words.

"I can't pretend to know why God chooses to save some and not others, but I do know my faith has taught me that His will is infallible, no matter how much I may not understand it. And right now, His will is that your existence should come to an end as you know it."

The sun had set behind us and the evening was almost completely covered in darkness, but I could see fear burning bright in Melana's eyes. Feeling detached from my own body, I sensed myself fly toward her. In the same moment, I saw something in Miriam's left hand flash from her thigh directly into demon's abdomen behind her. The alarm in Melana's eyes faded to pain as she collapsed to her knees behind Miriam. Taken by surprise, her claws fell to hang limply at her sides without doing Miriam any damage. I landed next to the demoness and plunged my knife into her throat as deeply as I could.

I heard the blood gurgle in her mouth. Melana's eyes went wide with shock and her body slumped to the ground.

"Miriam! Miriam, are you okay?" I swung around to examine my sister.

"Yes, baby. Where's Shad?"

"He's hurt bad, Miriam. You need to get him out of here. How's your arm? Can you still Jump?"

"I can Jump, Rose, but it's you I'm taking out of here first. I'll come right back for Shad."

I hesitated for only a second. "I'm not leaving, Miriam."

"Yes. You. Are. I'm taking you out of here now while I still can."

I knelt next to Miriam and searched for the words that would make her understand. I couldn't leave before I found Ouriel. I had to see him. *I have to know if*—I shook off that thought and the accompanying shiver before they could take root and fill me with despair.

"Miriam, I know I'm young. And I know I'm nearly defenseless. But I can't leave."

"You have no choice in the matter!"

"I know. But listen, Miri. Please!" I knew she wanted to interrupt, but my sister kept silent. "Could you leave without Shad? Without even knowing if he was dead or alive?"

Miriam looked away and didn't answer. I could see her resolve eroding, and the rest of my plea gushed out. "I can't leave Ouriel! Please! It would be like leaving one half of myself here to die. I'm already doing that with Ishmael. Don't make me do it with Ouri, too. He's alive. He has to be—" My voice broke with the strain of pleading with her, and Miriam's face softened.

"You're right. It's just that—you're my baby, and I've spent so long protecting you that I don't know if I can stop now."

"Please! Don't make me leave him."

I knew her answer as soon as the heartbreak registered on her face.

"Okay. I won't make you leave him, baby. I'm going to let you stay. You've proven yourself mature enough, and, whether you realize it or not, powerful enough to do this."

"Thank you," I sniffled into Miriam's shoulder, and she nearly collapsed from the ferocity my hug.

"Ow! You're welcome."

"I'm sorry! I forgot about your arm."

"That's okay. Now help me up and get me to Shad."

I grabbed Miriam's good arm and half-pulled, half-lifted her to her feet. We stumbled to where Shad lay, and Miriam fell to the ground by his side when she saw how badly he'd been injured.

"He'll be all right," I assured her. "The Healers will fix him. I promise." I helped her lay next to him on her good side. I made sure both her arms were wrapped around him and the rest of their bodies had close contact before I knelt to kiss her goodbye. "I love you, Miriam. And thank you. I'll do my best to stay alive. I promise."

"You better. I need you, baby sister." She smiled at me through her tears. "I love you, too. And, Rose—I know you can do this."

Miriam's words pierced me like the tears that were needling to the surface in my eyes.

"Thank you." I watched her and Shad mist away.

I was alone now and scared completely out of my senseless mind. A nagging pain in my right leg was just beginning to push itself forward in my consciousness. I looked down and was surprised to see a small, gaping wound in my thigh. I stifled a half sob, knowing it would do me no good to start feeling sorry for myself. I had to find Ouriel and get us out of this literally Godforsaken place.

Only the thought of him could have made me stand up and look for my weapons. I found my bow broken beneath the bodies of the demons that had attacked Shadrach and hoped the other Warriors would show up soon to set those two afire. I shivered at the thought of being chased down by two nasty demons with gaping wounds in their necks, dripping putrefied blood. The possibility totally grossed me out. With my bow useless, I turned to where I had left Melana lying with my knife in her throat.

She was gone.

With the knife Ouriel had told me never to be without.

Crap.

CHAPTER 12

I looked around and forced myself to focus. With only a small snort of self-derision, I found I had no idea where to go or what to do, until I noticed a small building directly behind the one I had just left. Obstructed from sight by the hulking mass of the others we had been working to clear, it connected to each of them by way of the metalwork that ran between the larger buildings.

Because I found no doors to the small building, I searched out the nearest outdoor stairs leading above. I limped my way up to and across the catwalk. Shuddering, I neared the previously hidden building. Malevolence poured from its doorway.

I strained to clear my thoughts. When I entered the small structure, a blinding darkness enveloped me, but I didn't panic. I could feel Ouriel close by, but just barely. I hoped I wouldn't be too late, like I had been with Ish. *No, I can't think about that.* His death was already too much for me to handle. A blast of grief hit me, but I pushed it aside. I had to keep moving forward. I felt my way around one corner, then another.

And I saw it.

My knees buckled with shock, and I fell to the floor. *It can't be*! My heart raced, and my stomach threatened to erupt. The information my eyes fed me had to be wrong.

The setting of my nightmare had come to life, and I knelt above it all.

From my vantage point, I saw the same gaping hole that had devoured my parents—the edges ragged and torn, as if part of the floor had collapsed into a room below. Rather than empty space, a bloody substance bubbled on its surface. The enormous pool rippled from time to time with what looked like horrible, scarred faces.

Its presence sucked the life from the room.

The bile in the back of my throat spewed out full force. It took a few minutes, but I finally quit retching. I stood and pried my eyes away from the reality of my dreams, and I almost fell again. Ouriel hung limply, just feet in front of me, suspended above the pool by a rope wrapped beneath his arms and around his chest.

I tried to grab hold of him from where I was standing, but he was just far enough away to be beyond my reach. Desperate to tear him down and check for signs of life, I had no idea how to get to him. Despite my panic, a strange awareness that he was still alive, but only barely, seeped into my consciousness. I heaved a small sigh of relief, only to realize that I was no longer alone with him.

"So, do you like my surprise?" a voice whispered close behind me. "I know this place holds such fond memories for you."

Battling the instinct to run, I turned slowly to confront the demon of my nightmares.

His hungry eyes noted every weakness, every doubt, in my soul. "Rose, my darling, how long I have waited for you!" Shockingly, I managed not to puke again when he leaned in close to me and sniffed my hair. "Ah, my sweet, sweet girl! Your soul Smells even more delicious than I could have dreamed. It is simply beautiful."

"You'll never get it, Ausen. I won't give it willingly," I shot back at him, even though I struggled with every word. My voice sounded confident and sure, echoing in the cavernous building, but I was drowning in terror. I had seen what this evil thing had done to my parents. But I'd never understood it had all been real. All those years, it hadn't been nightmares haunting me. I had Seen the deaths of my parents.

Actually Seen them.

I hadn't pieced those macabre images together from overheard conversations whispered behind my back as a heartbroken and orphaned child. Never could I have known every detail of this room from those conversations. The horrible stench that came to me with Ausen's every breath could in no way have been planted in my young mind thirteen years ago without my actually Seeing it.

The truth struck with such intensity I practically fell down the stairs behind me in an attempt to flee from it.

Shaken to the core, I stumbled down each step. I landed on the ground floor before I found enough courage to speak.

"Why have you brought me here, Ausen? Why have you gone to all this trouble? I can't save Ouriel. Hell! I didn't even know you weren't a figment of my childish imagination until just now. Anyone else would have been a better adversary in this sick game of yours. My soul is nowhere near powerful enough to satisfy you. You really should have set your sights higher. Ouriel's father, one of my sisters, surely they—"

"No, Rose, it is you. It has always been you."

"*What*? Why? Why do you want me, of all people? I am of a Guardian family, sure. But I can't really See. You've got to know that!" I fought to remain upright under the weight of my fear.

"Rose, Rose, Rose, but I don't know that. Tell me, are you really unaware, even after all you have done and Seen today?" Ausen paused for a moment, studying me. "I can't believe you don't know." He chuckled. "But you really *don't*, do you? I've watched you, in my own way, all of your life. I never bought into the act that you didn't know what you are. It seems I was wrong. Don't you wonder why I killed your parents that night?"

"They were Guardians. You wanted their souls, and they wouldn't surrender them to you. You thought you could threaten them with losing one of us. It's a prize for a demon to capture a Guardian's soul. My parents didn't give in, so you eliminated them." I had Seen that, in my dream, just before they died. *Right*? Or could Ausen have really wanted something else?

His shout of laughter came close to knocking me down. I managed to catch myself by grabbing hold of a shelf jutting from the wall. I came face to face with horrors in jars but jerked away before my mind could register what they were.

"I never wanted your parents' souls—well, no more than any other Guardian's anyway." He straightened the atrocities I had disturbed on his shelf then turned to me and smiled—a terrifying sight that nearly wilted me on the spot. "No, dear. I wanted you."

"*Me*?" I croaked, willing it not to be true. "But I was four! What could you have wanted with a four-year-old girl?"

"Demons can still See, once they've made the change. We keep all the Gifts we were created with, and we get a new one along with the transformation—the ability to Smell." Ausen took a step closer to me and those horrible nostrils of his dilated. "We Smell souls. And some of us—a precious few of us—are gifted with the ability to Smell every thought, word, and emotion that comprise a person's essence."

"And, what? Mine smells really good or something?" I sniffed with a bravado I didn't really feel. My only defense was to bluff my way through the situation I'd landed in. I had no special skills or powers to commend me. Even if I could See a little, I remained thoroughly ordinary. The only thing I had ever Seen, apparently, was my parents' death. Unfortunately, I had only just figured that out.

Heaven help me! Ouriel is doomed.

"There's no need to get smart with me. And, yes, it does, in fact, smell good, but not for the reason you think." Ausen paused, choosing his words with great care before he spoke again. "You see, this started the day your parents died. When you ran away, remember? They wouldn't let you read their Sacred Books, as I recall. You were ever so eager to begin your Guardian training, but they wouldn't let you. So you packed your little suitcase and left for...what was it? The circus?"

"No, I wanted to join the Convent down the street from our house. I thought, because I hadn't learned how to See yet, I could at least serve some greater purpose there." How did Ausen know all this? And it didn't have anything to do with my nightmare.

Did it?

"Yes, you always did crave becoming a noble servant of God, didn't you, silly girl? All that power, and you want to waste it on the greater good." Ausen broke off and shook his head. "Anyway, before your parents could find you—they were terrified, by the way—you crossed the path of a demon. Lucky for you, she was weak and knew you were of Guardian blood. That is the only reason you are alive today. She didn't know if she was strong enough to take on a Guardian, even a child as young as you were. She had been assigned to watch your family's house from your birth four years earlier. We wanted information on what powers the new Guardian child of your mother's bloodline may or may not bring to the Endless War.

"You had so naïvely gone out without protection, for once, and she was able to get close to you. Four years it took us to achieve that feat, and, from that moment on, your fate was sealed. You see, I've always had the special talent of being able to instantly Smell anything other demons Smell, so your scent was immediately passed from her demon mind to mine. And, at that moment, *you* became mine."

"Yours?" I still didn't understand how my parents' death was my fault. *What could be so special about me*? "I can't even See, Ausen!"

"Oh, sweet child, you can do so much more than See!"

Ausen's nonsensical speech had succeeded in distracting me from my main objective—saving Ouriel. I needed to regain some control over the situation, but I didn't know how. All the books, movies, and television I used to occupy my life had my subconscious shouting at me to keep Ausen talking. *Distract him*, I told myself, *while you think of something.* My eyes flicked around the room, searching out any possible escape, and caught a flash of something silver.

Ouriel's sword.

With a stupid plan in mind, I challenged Ausen. "Why are you being so mysterious? If you know so much about me, why don't you tell me exactly what it is I can do?"

"It's true that I hadn't counted on you not knowing anything," he mused. "And if you don't know at least something, this won't be nearly as much fun as I had planned. I have waited patiently these thirteen years—"

"Would you stop with all that cryptic crap?" Needling an insane demon had to be akin to poking a caged bear, but what did it matter? I was drowning in danger anyway. "Just what is it that makes this soul of mine smell so freaking magically delicious?"

I edged my way around the room toward the blade, careful to make my movements look like the results of fear. Absurdly, though, the question still remained—once I had the thing, what was I going to do with it? I totally sucked with a sword.

"You see, it is power that attracts demons most."

"Are you saying I have power? I can assure you I don't. You really should have tried for one of my sisters. Although, they're not as stupid as I am. They would never have fallen into your trap."

Ausen pursued my retreat, as I stumbled and cowered closer to the sword. I only had a few more feet to go.

"Oh, no! Neither of them would do. I want you. You alone have power that no human, Guardian or not, has ever thought possible. Seeing may not be your strength, but you have greater Gifts—"

I dove for Ouriel's sword. In one swift motion, I brought the blade to rest at Ausen's neck.

Unruffled by my display of force, he laughed. "A demon can only be killed by a Warrior, Rose. You know that."

"But I can cause you some serious damage." I smiled what I hoped was a wicked smile. "And I don't see you as the type who wants to carry his head around like a handbag."

Ausen sneered at me. "You haven't the strength."

In a move almost too fast for me to see, Ausen knocked the sword out of my hand and onto the floor. When I leaped after it, he knocked me headfirst into the far wall with one blow of his slimy arm. Curled up on the floor and in too much pain to move, I watched as he strode toward me. All I could see through my tangled hair was the claws on his feet.

"I don't want to hurt you." Ausen crouched down next to me. I didn't cringe when he flicked the hair out of my eyes. "I want you to be mine. I now control the entire demon horde, and you will become my consort. You have no need to be with this paltry Warrior. You deserve more. You deserve me."

I squelched my rising panic. "Do you seriously believe I would ever agree to that?"

"I do. I have someone you hold dear suspended just above the same portal that claimed the lives of your parents. One easy Jump and he is gone forever. Just. Like. Them." Ausen jerked me up and took flight. He carried me near enough to see Ouriel's labored breathing and smell the blood and sweat in his long hair. He was still unconscious. "Choose me, Rose. Take me for eternity, and you shall never die. Human trivialities will be nothing to you. Give me your soul. I do not want to consume it. I want to own it."

He glided down and dropped me at the pool's edge. I tried not to focus on the scarred, bubbling forms of those he had tortured before me. Instead, I turned and looked up at Ouriel.

Did he know about this power I supposedly had? Was it possible that he had known but never told me about this thing that Ausen seemed to know? Is that why so many lives had been risked to protect me?

Anger at the deception burned through me, but something even more powerful began to build in my body. I stared at Ouriel dangling helplessly above the bloody pool and swore he would not become one of those agonized souls like my parents.

I would not allow it.

"You will never have me." I stood and faced a waiting Ausen with defiance. "Not my soul and not as your consort. I am a Guardian, Sightless or not, and my destiny—from this moment on—will be to destroy you."

Fear flickered across Ausen's face but was quickly concealed. "You can't kill me! That is how it was written, determined, in the Sacred Books."

Ausen's fear fed my sense of power. "I *will* destroy you, Ausen. And if you want me as your consort, I must have something you fear."

"You don't know that. You don't even know what you're capable of, silly human." He leaned his towering body over me. "I will kill your little Warrior boyfriend if you don't agree to be mine."

"I will never be yours!"

Ausen soared upward. He neared Ouriel and reached out with a sharp claw to cut the rope holding my Warrior. I screamed, and the pool surged toward the demon. A bloody arm formed, snagged Ausen's ankle, and pulled him down. Desperate to escape being hauled into the melee of tortured souls, Ausen cut himself free with a swipe of his nail. He surged higher, and the twisted appendage fell away, lifeless.

"How did you do that?" Ausen shrieked from somewhere near the ceiling.

"Do what?"

"Those damned to the pool have never gotten so close to breaking free before! How did you do it?"

I hadn't done anything, but I wasn't about to admit it. "Isn't that just one of my many powers you know so much about?"

"You're bluffing. You didn't know you could do that." Ausen circled closer to Ouriel. "I wonder if you could repeat it."

He dove, and the pool reached for him again. This time, the groping arm missed. The souls and I had misjudged the demon's direction. Instead of Ouriel, Ausen lunged for me. He used my body as a shield to deflect the disembodied limb. It couldn't reach for him without ensnaring me.

Ausen pricked my right temple with his cold, spiky claw.

"Give. Me. Your. Soul." His voice rang with deathly calm, and his talon rested like the muzzle of a gun against my skin. "I see now that you are too powerful. Come to me willingly, or you will die."

"I won't do it."

"You will because, if you do not, your Warrior will follow you into the Pool of the Damned as soon as you're dead. If you come to me willingly, however, I will still allow him to go free."

I didn't know how to respond. My sisters were trained for this. For generations, my entire family had fought these battles. But I couldn't See. I had nothing left with which to fight.

"Give me your soul or you both will die."

Alone and lost, I turned to the only power left to me. I closed my eyes and the Guardian mantra chimed in my head. "God will protect me and I shall not fear. God will protect me and I shall not fear. *God will protect me and I shall not fear!*"

For the first time in my life, I felt true faith. It rushed through me and around me. It filled me.

And I could See.

The energy of every living thing in the room clamored for my attention. First, and foremost, I Saw Ouriel. I felt his every breath. I Saw his every thought. He had no lasting injuries, and his consciousness was alert and aware under whatever power Ausen was using to keep his body suppressed.

I also felt Ausen. He was scared—scared in a way he had never been before. Evil radiated from him in enormous waves, threatening my sanity.

Above what I sensed from Ouriel and Ausen, I felt the souls trapped in the pool. Their spirits rushed to embrace me and add their strength to my own. They swirled around me, and the air grew almost too thick to breathe. I opened my eyes and saw that the liquid from the pool had misted red to fill the room with swirling, constricting bodies. They were mine to control and command.

"Take him," I whispered.

Ausen screamed as his own victims clawed him away from me, dragging him back into the depths of the Damned with them. They tore at his wings, his legs, and his arms. He tried to scramble up and away from them, but the souls spiraled with him into the air and encircled him like a whirlpool, sucking him down below the surface. Just before his head went under, Ausen's eyes met mine, and I heard his mind scream, "They can't hold me forever. You *will* be mine." I joined my will with those of the scarred souls, and he was gone—lost in the abyss of his own Pool of the Damned.

Breathing heavily, I sank down beside the Pool. "May I ask one more favor of you?"

The answer came back a resounding "Yes!"

"Please—please—will you help me get him down?" I gestured toward Ouriel.

At once, the liquid swirled up again, freed Ouriel, and laid him gently next to me on the floor. The mist eased back toward the pool, and I murmured, "I swear, by all that is Holy, I will find the way to free you. If it exists, I will find it and do it."

In return, I heard only a sweet, "We know," and the pool calmed.

I pulled Ouriel's head onto my lap. "Ouriel!" I shook him gently. "Ouri, can you hear me?"

He didn't move.

I closed my eyes again and reached for the power I now knew lived inside me. I placed my hands on his stomach, as he had done for me not so long ago. My mind sought out both his spirit and the faith I finally understood.

The power of the Creator flowed through me into Ouriel. I focused all my energy and love on leading his mind back from wherever Ausen had pushed it. I felt a familiar explosion rock my body, and Ouriel and I were floating together in that same hazy nowhere as we had when he'd healed me.

I threw myself at him, and he snatched me into a tight embrace. Our lips met, and I felt the fire that raced through his body as well as I could feel my own.

"Rose!" He broke away from me. "You found your power."

The fog lifted, and I crashed back into the present. The putrid smell of the room and the Pool singed my nostrils. I looked for Ouriel and found his head still cradled in my lap, but his eyes were open and full of wonder.

"You knew!" I didn't want to believe it. "You always knew."

My accusation hit Ouriel, and the line of his mouth hardened. "Yes. I knew."

"How could you keep this from me?" The lump in my throat tasted like a strange mix of hurt, betrayal, and rage. "You knew all along who was after me and why."

Ouriel closed his eyes. "No, I did not know who. I have always known why, however."

"And you didn't tell me?" I couldn't keep the raw agony, the sense of loss, out of that statement. He had always known what I was. And yet, even now, I still wasn't sure *who* I was.

Ouriel's jaw clenched, and his eyes remained tightly shut. "I could not. It was forbidden. But I tried to do everything I could to prepare you."

"Look at me! And tell me why—"

Ouriel met my frown with one of his own. "Why, what, Rose?"

"Why me? Why you? I don't understand any of this. What does it all mean?"

"The answers to your first two questions are simple. My family was charged with protecting yours at the birth of the first Guardians, and your matrilineal bloodline has produced the greatest Guardians throughout history."

"Your family?" Yet another betrayal. "Ishmael–he's your uncle, and you never told me."

"I couldn't! You first had to learn to See. On your own. No one could force it on you. The Sacred Books are terribly clear on that point."

"But why your family? Why mine?"

"What is my name?" Ouriel asked gently.

"Ouriel. Ouriel San Miguel."

He looked at me expectantly, and something struggled to come forward in my mind. Why would his name be important?

"Rose, you are bilingual, are you not?" Ouriel smirked.

It finally hit me. St. Michael, as in the archangel, had to be Ouriel's grandfather or something. That was why his family was so prominent in the War. Why Ouriel himself was so powerful. "He was your grandfather, wasn't he?"

Ouriel nodded. "He *is* my grandfather. And he very desperately wants to meet you."

"Me?" I squeaked. I took a deep breath and tried to order my thoughts. It felt like Ouriel wanted to distract me from something. Something infinitely more important. What was it?

"Okay, that's your family. You didn't tell me why mine was chosen."

Ouriel grimaced. "I do not know if you want to hear it."

"Tell me."

"Rose—"

"Ouriel, so help me—I'm done with secrets. Tell me now before I scream!" I was through being lied to.

"All right." Ouriel sighed. "It goes all the way back to the origin of the Guardians. You know already that the Edomites, Esau's descendants, had turned almost entirely to following Helel. What you don't know is your grandfather, however many generations removed, was their king. He committed great abominations in the eyes of the Lord.

He murdered his wife and almost all of his children when they refused to abandon Elohim.

"One daughter alone survived. She was given to Ishmael to protect, and he guarded her until she came of age to fight. She chose a powerful husband and a few others to join the two of them as the first Guardians. It was she who wrote the Sacred Books. It was she whom the Lord entrusted with the duty of protecting innocent human life. This is the basic history all Guardians are taught.

"What they are not taught and what only we, the descendants of Michael, God's beloved and vanquisher of Helel, know is that her direct line was prophesied to bring forth the one Guardian who could bring balance to the War and possibly end it altogether."

My mind almost cracked under the strain. I knew the truth, without a doubt, before I said the words. "It's me isn't it? I'm the one."

"Yes, Rose. It is you."

His simple words were like a blow to my stomach. I didn't want to hear my greatest fear confirmed—especially from the only lips that had ever touched mine. I had never wanted to fight.

All I'd ever wanted was to live in peace—and to love Ouriel.

But none of that could be now, so I swallowed my tears, my anger, and my heart.

I squeezed in one last question before I fell apart. "What was her name?"

"An ancient form of Rose."

The room went black, and I felt Ouriel catch me before my head cracked on the concrete floor.

EPILOGUE

R ose?" Miriam's voice beckoned me softly.
I had no idea how long I'd been in bed. Days—
definitely. Weeks—maybe. Time was a total
blur. I had no desire to talk to anyone, not even Ouriel. I
only cared that my sisters and brother-in-law were okay
and that both Gen and Shad had recovered well. Gen was
up and about like she had never been injured, but Shad
still hobbled around the house only with the help of a
cane. And, sadly, I couldn't even work up the will to
tease him about it.

I had stayed in my room as much as I was allowed
after the confrontation with Ausen—and Ishmael's
death—and staunchly refused to see anyone but my family. Ouriel had strict orders to remain out of sight, and I
had been spared the agony of a funeral for Ishmael thus

far. A memorial service for all who had been lost in the battle was planned for some time in the near future—again, I had no idea when—to take place as soon as the survivors were all well enough to attend.

Miriam's insistent voice snapped me back into the present. "Rose, someone is here to see you."

"I don't want to see anyone. Tell whoever it is to go away." I looked up from my bed to see her hesitating in my doorway. "Leave me alone, Miri. Please."

I re-buried my face in my pillow.

"Young one, your sister loves you and is terribly worried for you," a gentle, booming voice advised.

I looked up to give the Mufasa sound-alike a quick, "Get lost!" but forgot the words at the sight of a huge, ancient Warrior filling my room. I swallowed hard.

"You're him—you're Ouriel's grandfather," I whispered, awed, while Miriam slipped away.

"Yes, little one." He smiled. "I am Michael. There is no need to preface my name with any titles or appendage it with the term archangel, seeing as my grandson loves you so desperately."

I felt my face blanch with guilt. Ouriel had been waiting out my depression—or tantrum as Gen called it—for days while living in our guesthouse.

"I see the mere mention of him pains you." He smiled at me again. "You must love him as well."

I looked at the legendary Warrior, standing in my messy, ridiculous teenage room, and found I couldn't lie to him. My skill suddenly eluded me. Rather than tell him how right he was, though, I kept my mouth stubbornly shut.

"Ah—you are a tough one, are you not? The Creator always amazes me with creations far more beautiful than my imaginings." St. Michael—it was difficult not to think of him without the title—stopped for a moment to study me in silence. "Yes—you are beautiful beyond anything I could have thought possible. No wonder Ouriel was lost to you long ago. I wonder, do you know just how long the boy has loved you?" He waited for my answer and, when he saw I wasn't going to give one, continued, "He has loved you most of your life. It was he who rescued you the day you ran away from home at the age of four. It was he who found you when no one else could.

"Throughout the nightmare that followed, you would not allow anyone else near you. He remained at your side during all of it. He was the one who held you after you woke from your first vision. It was he who realized who you were. He was also the first to see that the horror of Seeing your parents' death, and knowing that you were at the root of it, caused you to repress any and every form of your gift.

"He was ordered shortly thereafter to the Middle East to lead an operation there. Upon his return, he realized that you had no recollection of him and felt that having his presence forced upon you would only worsen your situation. He determined then to stay away from you. His only consolation was being given command of your guard—as he remains today. You see, your love for one another was apparent long ago, although neither of you knew it. I believe it was predetermined."

"But I thought that God gave us free will."

The Warrior chuckled. "That He did, my dear, and it is a principle you are demonstrating admirably well right now by remaining shut up in your room rather than facing your destiny."

I wanted to lash out and scream at him, but an argument with St. Michael would be impossible. *Seriously— how* does *a person fight with an archangel?* All my excuses, all of my anger, crumbled in the face of such a perfect, amazing creature. Only fear and a deep, deep sorrow remained in their place.

"Why did God choose *me* to do this?" I cried out, despair ripping through my voice. "I'm tired of being me. I don't want to do any of this anymore!"

"Darling child," St. Michael cooed, as he picked me up and pressed my head to his shoulder. "None of us ever knows why the Creator chooses us. We know only that we must answer His call."

"But I don't want to—I just—I want my mother! Or my father. And I want Ishmael back. I can't stand it anymore!" I sobbed into his shoulder.

"I know, my sweet. I know. Who is there to know better than I? Do you think I cherished forcing my brother—my elder brother at that—from the presence of our Father? He was bigger, stronger, braver, than I ever was, but he was also more prideful, more arrogant, and more evil. In the end, I found the most difficult part of the battle was its mental, not its physical, aspect. I could not rely merely upon my faith in the Father but also had to trust in His faith in me. We are not given that which we cannot bear. In the end, I was what He trusted me to be, as you will be also."

How could I be this person they all expected me to be? "But I don't feel like I will be. I am nothing. I have always been nothing, and I was actually glad of it."

"Rose, we all kick, scream, and stomp our feet at the path God has laid before us, but, in the end, we hoist our crosses on our backs and drag it in the direction He shows us. You will do the same. You won't refuse it. The ability is not in you. You have never been one to deny God. You will not start now, even if it takes you a moment of rebellion to figure it out."

I recognized the truth in his words, but I just wanted a little more time—for stolen innocence, hidden youth— before I turned down a road that would rob me of both. Realizing they were already lost to me, I knew only one question remained to be asked.

"Now that—" I choked on the words, "that Ish is gone, can you see him again? You know, go to…wherever he is now?"

St. Michael clutched me tighter to him for just a moment. Gently, he set me next to him on the bed and turned toward the wall. I could see the muscles working in his jaw before he spoke.

"I am afraid that seeing Ishmael now is beyond even me. Certain celestial realms are not meant for those who bloody themselves with the terrestrial." His eyes seemed to search for something in the air that I couldn't see. He sighed and dropped his head into his large hands. "No. I will never see my beloved firstborn again."

We sat in silence and shared grief for a few more seconds before St. Michael finally stood. "There remains only one task to me now, my dear. I must ask that you end my grandson's suffering. He is a great Warrior, but you and he are now so intertwined that he can no longer function with such antagonism emanating from you. He will leave if you ask him to, and he will live his life without you if he must. Whatever choice you make, however you choose to proceed from this moment, find him a way to do so in peace, I beg you."

I could only nod in response.

"I will send him in to you." St. Michael kissed me gently on the forehead and walked out of my room.

I hadn't seen Ouriel since I fainted the night of Ishmael's death. My heart pounded, and I tried not to freak out. I didn't know what I was going to say to him, and I really didn't know what I wanted from him.

I knew only two things for sure—I was more in love with Ouriel than I had ever thought it possible to love anyone and now I had no idea who I was anymore. The world I lived in was no longer the world I thought I'd known.

How—how could I be with Ouriel, love Ouriel, when I didn't even know myself? It was as if I woke up one day, thinking I knew everything about my life and where it was going, only to find myself lost down my own personal rabbit hole.

How could I promise him anything anymore? The way I felt for him seemed like it promised forever. So did his feelings for me, but how could I follow through on that if I was nothing more than a figurative toddler rediscovering the world around her?

I loved Ouriel—even more than I imagined he could possibly love me. For that reason alone, I knew what decision I needed to make.

I had to step away from him. I couldn't stop loving him, but I could stay far enough away that I might be able to find myself—to come to know myself.

He deserved that. He deserved a woman who came to him whole and with the knowledge of who she was entirely. Not some teenager floundering, lost and broken, in the life thrust upon her.

I heard a sound at the door and looked up to see Ouriel framed by the light streaming down the hallway. The sight of him broke my heart.

His color had faded to a pasty peach, and he had lost weight.

He stood, hesitant, at my door. "Rose?" The sound of despair in his voice was almost palpable.

"Ouriel," I whispered. I couldn't remember what I had resolved in the moment before he came into my room. All rational thought had left me. In its absence, I felt only my love for the proud, brave Warrior.

I reached for him, and he gathered me hungrily into his arms. His mouth found mine, and his rough kiss consumed me. I was lost in it. I couldn't recover my senses

THE BROKEN   239

until he pulled away and touched my face softly with his fingertips.

His tenderness undid me.

I began to sob. Great heaving breaths racked my body. I knew I couldn't pick up with him where our relationship had left off. It would never be the same. No longer was ours an innocent infatuation. It had grown overnight into a mature, forever kind of love. That fact made it almost impossible, but totally necessary, for me to say what was in my heart.

"Ouriel—" I almost couldn't speak through my incessant sobs. "Ouriel, I can't! I can't have you risk your life for me ever again."

"It is my sacred duty."

"I know that!" I snapped. "And don't feed me that duty crap! I can't stand it right now. I don't want you in danger."

"Nor I you." He sighed. "You cannot push me away with worries for my safety. Even if it were not my duty, my love for you would always lead me into danger to protect you. Or fight beside you, if that were the case."

"I know." I fought for control of my emotions. "After I saw Ishmael, and when I thought you might be dead too—dead because you were helping me—well, I almost lost my mind. I don't know if I could ever live through that again."

"Rose, I will continue to fight. With or without you. Always. That is my nature. You cannot stop me or forbid me to do so."

The burden of his words nearly crushed me with their undeniable truth. I'd always known that Ouriel's dying might be a real possibility, but I couldn't deal with it so soon after losing Ishmael.

And so I said it quickly, in one breath, like ripping off a bandage, "I'm not ready for all of this Ouriel. Not for us, not for my Gifts, not for the fight I know is coming." I couldn't stop the sobs that resurfaced as I pried myself out of his arms—the very arms that I wanted to hold me more than anything.

"I know, my sweet. I have always known."

His gentle understanding was another knife in my already shredded heart. I wanted him to be angry with me, to storm out of my life—to do anything that would make it easier to blame him for what was about to come out of my mouth.

"Rose, say what you must, so I may say what I must."

I drew a deep breath and prepared to break his heart—possibly irreparably—and my own in the process.

"Ouri." I reached out and grabbed hold of his warm hands. "I love you, and I always will. But how can I promise you my love forever when I'm not even old enough to know what forever is?"

"I love you, too." Ouriel brought my hands to his lips and kissed my fingertips. "And I will wait for you to understand fully what it means to commit yourself to me forever. I will wait for you, Rose. Quietly and patiently. I will remain by your side—as a guide and protector only—until the time is right. And when it is, you will be mine. Forever."

With that, Ouriel, as he was wont to do, strode out of my room without looking back.

And I gaped after him, loving him more than ever.

THE END
(for now)

About the Author

Julia Joseph taught Theatre for nine years in Texas middle and high schools, where she wrote and produced three original plays for her students. In 2011, Joseph left teaching to devote all of her energy to her own children and to writing a novel. She earned her B. A. in English Literature and Language with a focus in Drama from St. Mary's University in San Antonio, Texas.

Joseph spends most of her free time reading, writing, and chauffeuring her kids between activities. She lives happily with her husband and two children wherever the Army happens to station them.

71252977R00142

Made in the USA
Columbia, SC
23 May 2017